S0-ACP-612

ENTHUSIASTIC ACCLAIM FOR A CRIME FICTION
GIANT—*NEW YORK TIMES* BESTSELLING
GRAND MASTER

TONY HILLERMAN

"Hillerman is a master."
St. Louis Post-Dispatch

"Surely one of the finest and
most original craftsmen."
Boston Globe

"Hillerman transcends the mystery genre."
Washington Post Book World

"What he communicates better than almost any
other suspense writer is a different sense of time,
a different sense of connection to nature,
a different way of being."
Ft. Worth Star-Telegram

"An amazing writer."
Albuquerque Journal

"Hillerman's novels are like no others."
San Diego Union-Tribune

"His Leaphorn/Chee series is one of the most
original and influential in modern crime fiction."
Portland Sunday Oregonian

"We couldn't do better for a true voice of the West."
Denver Rocky Mountain News

BOOKS BY TONY HILLERMAN

FICTION
The Shape Shifter
Skeleton Man • *The Sinister Pig*
The Wailing Wind • *Hunting Badger*
The First Eagle • *The Fallen Man*
Finding Moon • *Sacred Clowns*
Coyote Waits • *Talking God*
A Thief of Time • *Skinwalkers*
The Ghostway • *The Dark Wind*
People of Darkness • *Listening Woman*
Dance Hall of the Dead • *The Fly on the Wall*
The Blessing Way • *The Mysterious West*
The Boy Who Made Dragonfly (for children)
Buster Mesquite's Cowboy Band (for children)

NONFICTION
Seldom Disappointed
Hillerman Country
The Great Taos Bank Robbery
Rio Grande
New Mexico
The Spell of New Mexico
Indian Country
Talking Mysteries (with Ernie Bulow)
Kilroy Was There
A New Omnibus of Crime

NOW AVAILABLE IN HARDCOVER
Tony Hillerman's Landscape by Anne Hillerman

ATTENTION: ORGANIZATIONS AND CORPORATIONS
Most Harper paperbacks are available at special quantity discounts
for bulk purchases for sales promotions, premiums, or fund-raising.
For information, please call or write:

Special Markets Department, HarperCollins Publishers,
10 East 53rd Street, New York, New York 10022-5299.
Telephone: (212) 207-7528.   Fax: (212) 207-7222.

HUNTING BADGER

TONY HILLERMAN

HARPER

An Imprint of HarperCollinsPublishers

This is a work of fiction. Names, characters, places, and incidents are products of the author's imagination or are used fictitiously and are not to be construed as real. Any resemblance to actual events, locales, organizations, or persons, living or dead, is entirely coincidental.

HARPER

An Imprint of HarperCollins*Publishers*
10 East 53rd Street
New York, New York 10022-5299

Copyright © 1999 by Tony Hillerman
ISBN 978-0-06-196782-5

All rights reserved. No part of this book may be used or reproduced in any manner whatsoever without written permission, except in the case of brief quotations embodied in critical articles and reviews. For information address Harper paperbacks, an Imprint of HarperCollins Publishers.

First Harper premium paperback printing: October 2010
First HarperTorch paperback printing: January 2001
First HarperCollins hardcover printing: November 1999

HarperCollins® and Harper® are registered trademarks of Harper-Collins Publishers.

Printed in the United States of America

Visit Harper paperbacks on the World Wide Web at
www.harpercollins.com

10 9 8 7 6 5 4 3 2

If you purchased this book without a cover, you should be aware that this book is stolen property. It was reported as "unsold and destroyed" to the publisher, and neither the author nor the publisher has received any payment for this "stripped book."

For Officer Dale Claxton
Who died doing his duty, bravely and alone

AUTHOR'S NOTE

On May 4, 1998, Officer Dale Claxton of the Cortez, Colorado, police stopped a stolen water truck. Three men in it killed him with a fusillade of automatic-weapons fire. In the ensuing chase, three other officers were wounded, one of the suspects killed himself, and the two survivors vanished into the vast, empty wilderness of mountains, mesas, and canyons on the Utah-Arizona border. The Federal Bureau of Investigation took over the manhunt. Soon it involved more than five hundred officers from at least twenty federal, state, and tribal agencies, and bounty hunters attracted by a $250,000 FBI reward offer.

To quote Leonard Butler, the astute Chief of Navajo Tribal Police, the search "became a circus." Sighting reports sent to the coordinator were not reaching search teams. Search parties found themselves tracking one another, unable to communicate on mismatched radio frequencies, local police who knew the country sat at roadblocks while teams brought in from the cities were floundering in canyons strange to them. The town of Bluff was evacuated, a brush fire was set in the San Juan bottoms to smoke out the fugitives, and the hunt dragged on into the summer. The word spread in July that the FBI believed the fugitives dead (possibly of laughter, one of my cop friends said). By August, only the Navajo Police still had scouts out looking for signs.

As I write this (July 1999) the fugitives remain free. But the hunt of 1998 exists in this book only as the fictional memory of fictional characters.

Tony Hillerman

The characters in this book are fictional with the exception of Patti (P.J.) Collins and the Environmental Protection Agency survey team. My thanks to Ms. Collins for providing information about this radiation-mapping job, and to P.J. and the copter crew for giving Chee a ride up Gothic Canyon.

HUNTING BADGER

ONE

DEPUTY SHERIFF TEDDY Bai had been leaning on the doorframe looking out at the night about three minutes or so before he became aware that Cap Stoner was watching him.

"Just getting some air," Bai said. "Too damn much cigarette smoke in there."

"You're edgy tonight," Cap said, moving up to stand in the doorway beside him. "You young single fellas ain't supposed to have anything worrying you."

"I don't," Teddy said.

"Except maybe staying single," Cap said. "There's that."

"Not with me," Teddy said, and looked at Cap to see if he could read anything in the old man's expression. But Cap was looking out into the Ute Casino's parking lot, showing only the left side of his face, with its brush of white mustache, short-cropped white hair and the puckered scar left along the cheekbone when, as Cap told it, a woman he was arresting for Driving While Intoxicated fished a pistol out of her purse and shot him. That had been about forty years ago, when Stoner had been with the New Mexico State Police only a couple of years and had not yet learned that survival required skepticism about all his fellow humans. Now Stoner was a former captain, augmenting his retirement pay as a rent-a-cop security director at the Southern Ute gambling establishment—just as Teddy was doing on his off-duty nights.

"What'd ya tell that noisy drunk at the black-jack table?"

"Just the usual," Teddy said. "Calm down or he'd have to leave."

Cap didn't comment. He stared out into the night. "Saw some lightning," he said, pointing. "Just barely. Must be way out there over Utah. Time for it, too."

"Yeah," Teddy said, wanting Cap to go away.

"Time for the monsoons to start," Cap said. "The thirteenth, isn't it? I'm surprised so many people are out here trying their luck on Friday the thirteenth."

Teddy nodded, providing no fodder to extend this conversation. But Cap didn't need any.

"But then it's payday. They got to get rid of all that money in their pay envelopes." Cap looked at his watch. "Three-thirty-three," he announced. "Almost time for the truck to get here to haul off the loot to the bank."

And, Teddy thought, a few minutes past the time when a little blue Ford Escort was supposed to have arrived in the west lot. "Well," he said, "I'll go prowl around the parking areas. Scare off the thieves."

Teddy found neither thieves nor a little blue Escort in the west lot. When he looked back at the EMPLOYEES ONLY doorway, Cap was no longer there. A few minutes late. A thousand reasons that could happen. No big deal. He enjoyed the clean air, the predawn high-country chill, the occasional lightning over the mountains. He walked out of the lighted area to check his memory of the midsummer starscape. Most of the constellations were where he remembered they should be. He could recall their American names, and some of the names his Navajo grandmother had taught him, but only two of the names he'd wheedled out of his Kiowa-Comanche father. Now was that moment his grandmother called the "deep dark time," but the late-rising moon was causing a faint glow outlining the shape of Sleeping Ute Mountain. He heard the sound of laughter from somewhere. A car door slammed. Then another. Two vehicles pulled out of the east lot, heading for the exit. Coyotes began a conversation of yips and yodels among the piñons in the hills behind the casino. The sound of a truck gearing down came from the highway below. A pickup pulled into the EMPLOYEES ONLY lot, parked, produced the clattering sound of something being unloaded.

Teddy pushed the illumination button on his Timex. Three-forty-six. Now the little blue car was late enough to make him wonder a little. A man wearing what looked like coveralls emerged into the light carrying an extension ladder. He placed it against the casino wall, trotted up it to the roof.

"Now what's that about?" Teddy said, half aloud. Probably an electrician. Probably something wrong with the air-conditioning. "Hey," he shouted, and started toward the ladder. Another pickup pulled into the employee lot—this one a big oversize-cab job. Doors opened. Two men emerged. National Guard soldiers apparently, dressed in their fatigues. Carrying what? They were walking fast toward the EMPLOYEES ONLY door. But that door had no outside knob. It was the accounting room, opened only from the inside and only by guys as important as Cap Stoner.

Stoner was coming out of the side entrance now. He pointed at the roof, shouted, "Who's that up there? What the hell—"

"Hey," Teddy yelled, trotting toward the two men, unsnapping the flap on his holster. "What's—"

Both men stopped. Teddy saw muzzle flashes, saw Cap Stoner fall backward, sprawled on the pavement. The men spun toward him, swinging their weapons. He was fumbling with his pistol when the first bullets struck him.

TWO

SERGEANT JIM CHEE of the Navajo Tribal Police was feeling downright fine. He was just back from a seventeen-day vacation. He was happily reassigned from an acting-lieutenant assignment in Tuba City to his old Shiprock home territory, and he had five days of vacation left before reporting back to work. The leftover mutton stew extracted from his little refrigerator was bubbling pleasantly on the propane burner. The coffeepot steamed— producing an aroma as delicious as the stew. Best of all, when he did report for work there wouldn't be a single piece of paperwork awaiting his attention.

Now, as he filled his bowl and poured his coffee, what he was hearing on the early news made him feel even better. His fear—his downright dread— that he'd soon be involved in another FBI-directed backcountry manhunt was being erased. The TV announcer was speaking "live" from the Federal Courthouse, reporting that the bad guys who had robbed the casino on the Southern Ute Reservation about the time Chee was leaving Fairbanks were now "probably several hundred miles away."

In other words, safely out of Shiprock's Four Corners territory and too far away to be his problem.

The theory of the crime the FBI had hung on this robbery, as the handsome young TV employee was now reporting on the seventeen-inch screen in Chee's trailer, went like this: "Sources involved in the hunt said the three bandits had stolen a small single-engine aircraft from a ranch south of Montezuma Creek, Utah. Efforts to trace the plane are under way, and the FBI asked anyone who might have seen the plane yesterday or this morning to call the FBI."

Chee sampled the stew, sipped coffee and listened to the announcer describe the plane—an elderly dark blue single-engine high-wing monoplane—a type used by the U.S. Army for scouting and artillery spotting in Korea and the early years of the Vietnam War. The sources quoted suggested the robbers had taken the aircraft from the rancher's hangar and used it to flee the area.

That sounded good to Chee. The farther the better. Canada would be fine, or Mexico. Anywhere but the Four Corners. In the spring of 1998 he'd been involved in an exhausting, frustrating FBI-directed manhunt for two cop killers. At its chaotic worst, officers from more than twenty federal, state, county and reservation agencies had floundered around for weeks in that one with no arrests made before the federals decided to call it off by declaring the suspects "probably dead." It wasn't an experience Chee wanted to repeat.

The little hatch Chee had cut into the bottom of the trailer door clattered behind him on its rubber hinges, which meant his cat was making an un-usually early visit. That told Chee that a coyote was close enough to make Cat nervous or a visitor was coming. Chee listened. Over the sound of the television, now selling a cell-telephone service, he heard wheels on the dirt track that connected his home under the San Juan River cottonwoods to the Shiprock-Cortez highway above.

Who would it be? Maybe Cowboy Dashee, but this wasn't Cowboy's usual day off from his deputy sheriff's job. Chee swallowed another bite of stew, went to the door and pulled back the curtain. A fairly new Ford 150 pickup rolled to a stop under the nearest tree. Officer Bernadette Manuelito was sitting in it, staring straight ahead. Waiting, Navajo fashion, for him to recognize her arrival.

Chee sighed. He was not ready for Bernie. Bernie represented something he'd have to deal with sooner or later, but he preferred later. The gossip in the small world of cops had it that Bernie had a crush on him. Probably true, but not something he wanted to think about now. He'd wanted some time. Time to adjust to the joy of being demoted from acting lieutenant back to sergeant. Time to get over the numbness of knowing he'd finally burned the bridge that had on its other end Janet Pete—seductive, smart, chic, sweet and treacherous. He wasn't ready for another problem. But he opened the door.

Officer Manuelito seemed to be off-duty. She climbed out of her truck wearing jeans, boots, a red shirt and a Cleveland Indians baseball cap and looking small, pretty and slightly untidy, just as he remembered her. But somber. Even her smile had a sad edge to it. Instead of the joke he had ready for her, Chee simply invited her in, gesturing to his chair beside the table. He sat on the edge of his cot and waited.

"Welcome back to Shiprock," Bernie said.

"Happy to escape from Tuba," Chee said. "How's your mother?"

"About the same," Bernie said. Last winter, her mother's drift into the dark mists of Alzheimer's disease won Officer Manuelito a transfer back to Shiprock, where she could better care for her. Chee's was a late-summer transfer, caused by his reversion from acting lieutenant to sergeant. The

Tuba City section didn't need another sergeant. Shiprock did.

"Terrible disease," Chee said.

Bernie nodded. Glanced at him. Looked away.

"I heard you went up to Alaska," Bernie said. "How was it?"

"Impressive. Took the cruise up the coast." He waited. Bernie hadn't made this call to hear about his vacation.

"I don't know how to do this," she said, giving him a sidelong glance.

"Do what?" Chee asked.

"You don't have anything to do with that casino thing, do you?"

Chee felt trouble coming. "No," he said.

"Anyway, I need some advice."

"I'd say just turn yourself in. Return the money. Make a full confession and . . ."

Chee stopped there, wishing he'd kept his mouth shut. Bernie was looking at him now, and her expression said this was not the time for half-baked humor.

"Do you know Teddy Bai?"

"Bai? Is that the rent-a-cop wounded in the casino robbery?"

"Teddy's a Montezuma County deputy sheriff," Bernie said, rather stiffly. "That was just a part-time temporary job with casino security. He was just trying to make some extra money."

"I wasn't—" Chee began and stopped. Less said the better until he knew what this was all about. So he said, "I don't know him." And waited.

"He's in the hospital at Farmington," Bernie said. "In intensive care. Shot three times. Once through a lung. Once through the stomach. Once through the right shoulder."

Clearly Bernie knew Bai pretty well. All he knew about this case personally was what he'd read in the papers, and he hadn't seen any of these details reported. He said, "Well, that San Juan Medical Center there has a good reputation. I'd think he'd be getting—"

"They think he was involved in the robbery," Bernie said. "I mean the FBI thinks so. They have a guard outside his room."

Chee said, "Oh?" And waited again. If Bernie knew why they thought that, she'd tell him. What he'd read, and what he'd heard, was that the bandits had killed the casino security boss and critically wounded a guard. Then, during their escape, they'd shot at a Utah Highway Patrolman who had flagged them for speeding.

Bernie looked close to tears. "It doesn't make any sense," she said.

"It doesn't seem to. Why would they want to shoot their own man?"

"They think Teddy was the inside man," Bernie said. "They think the robbers shot him because he knew who they were, and they didn't trust him."

Chee nodded. He didn't have to ask Bernie how she knew all this confidential stuff. Even if it wasn't her case, she was a cop, and if she really wanted to know, she'd know who to talk to. "Sounds pretty weak to me," he said. "Cap Stoner was shot, too. He was the security boss out there. You'd think they'd figure Stoner for the inside man."

He rose, poured a cup of coffee and handed it to Bernie, giving her a little time to think how she wanted to answer that.

"Everybody liked Stoner," she said. "All the old-timers anyway. And Teddy's been in trouble before," she said. "When he was just a kid. He got arrested for joyriding in somebody else's truck."

"Well it couldn't have been very serious," Chee said. "At least the county was willing to hire him as a deputy."

"It was a juvenile thing," Bernie said.

"Awful weak then. Do they have something else on him?"

"Not really," she said.

He waited. Bernie's expression told him something worse was coming. Or maybe not. Maybe she wouldn't tell him.

She sighed. "People at the casino said he'd been acting strange. They said he was nervous. Instead of watching people inside, he kept going out into the parking lot. When his shift was over, he stayed around. He told one of the cleanup crew he was waiting to be picked up."

"OK," Chee said. "I can see it now. I mean them thinking he was waiting for the gang to show up. In case they needed help."

"He wasn't, though. He was waiting for someone else."

"No problem, then. When he gets well enough to talk, he tells the feds who he was waiting for. They check, confirm it, and there's no reason to hold him," Chee said, thinking there was probably something else.

"I don't think he'll tell," Bernie said.

"Oh. You mean he was waiting for a woman then?" He didn't pursue that. Didn't ask her how she knew all this, or why she hadn't passed it along to the FBI. Didn't ask her why she had come here to tell him about it.

"I don't know what to do," Bernie said.

"Probably nothing," he said. "If you do, they'll want to know how you got this information. Then they'll talk to his wife. Mess up his marriage."

"He's not married."

Chee nodded, thinking there could be all sorts of reasons a guy wouldn't want the world to know about a woman picking him up at 4 A.M. He just couldn't think of a good one right away.

"They'll be trying to get him to tell who the robbers were," Bernie said. "They'll come up with some way to hold him until he tells. And he won't know who they are. So I'm afraid they'll find something to charge him with so they can hold him."

"I just got back from Alaska," Chee said, "so I don't know anything about any of this. But I'll bet they got a good idea by now who they're looking for."

Bernie shook her head. "No. I don't think so," she said. "I hear that's a total blank. They were talking at first like it was some of the right-wingers in one of the militia groups. Something political. But now I hear they don't have a clue."

Chee nodded. That would explain why the FBI had been so quick to announce the aircraft business. It took the heat off the area Agent in Charge.

"You're sure you know Bai was waiting for a woman? Do you know who?"

Bernie hesitated. "Yes."

"Could you tell the feds?"

"I guess I could. I will if I have to." She put the coffee cup on the table, untasted. "You know what I was thinking? I was thinking you worked here a long time before they shifted you to Tuba City. You know a lot of people. With the FBI thinking they already have the inside man they won't be looking for the real inside man. I thought maybe you could find out who really was their helper in the casino. If anybody can."

Now it was Chee's turn to hesitate. He sipped his coffee, cold now, and tried to sort out his mixture of reactions to all this. Bernie's confidence in him was flattering, if misguided. Why did the thought that Bernie was having an affair with this rent-a-cop disappoint him? It should be a relief. Instead it gave him an empty, abandoned feeling.

"I'll ask around," Chee said.

THREE

THE ONLY CLIENT in the dining room in Window Rock's Navajo Inn was sitting at a table in the corner with a glass of milk in front of him. He was wearing a droopy gray felt Stetson and reading the *Gallup Independent*. Joe Leaphorn stood at the entrance a moment studying him. Roy Gershwin, looking a lot older, more weather-beaten and worn-out than he'd remembered him. But then he hadn't seen him for years—not since Gershwin had helped him nail a U.S. Forest Service ranger who'd been augmenting his income by digging artifacts out of Anasazi burials on a Gershwin grazing lease. That had been at least six years ago, about the time Leaphorn had started thinking about retirement. But they went far back beyond that—back to Leaphorn's rookie years. Back to a summer when Leaphorn had arrested one of Gershwin's hired hands on a rape complaint—a bad start with a happy ending. That had been the first time he'd heard Gershwin's deep, gruff whiskey-ruined voice—an angry voice telling Leaphorn he'd arrested an innocent man. When he had answered the telephone this morning, he recognized that odd voice instantly.

"Lieutenant Leaphorn," Gershwin had said. "I hear you're retired now. Is that right? If it is, I guess I'm trying to impose on you."

"Mr. Gershwin," Leaphorn had replied. "It's Mr. Leaphorn now, and it's good to hear from you." He had heard himself saying that with a sort of surprise. This was what retirement was doing to him. And what lay ahead. This old rancher had never really been a friend. Just one of those thousands of people you deal with in a lifetime spent as a cop. But here he was, genuinely happy to hear his telephone ring. Happy to have someone to talk to.

But Gershwin had stopped talking. Long silence. The sound of the man clearing his throat. Then: "I guess this ain't going to surprise you much. I mean to tell you I got myself a problem. I guess you've heard that from a lot of people. Being a policeman."

"Sort of goes with the job," Leaphorn said. Two years ago he would have grumbled about this sort of call. Today he didn't. Loneliness conditions.

"Well," Gershwin said, "I got something I don't know how to handle. I'd like to talk to you about it."

"Let's hear it."

"I'm afraid it's not something you can handle over the telephone," Gershwin replied.

So they arranged to meet at three at the Navajo Inn. It was now three minutes short of that. Gershwin looked up, noticed Leaphorn approaching, stood and motioned him to the chair across from him.

"Damn good of you to come," he said. "I was afraid you'd tell me you were retired now and I should worry somebody else with it."

"Glad to help if I can," Leaphorn said. They polished off the required social formalities faster than usual, discussing the cold, dry winter, poor grazing, risk of forest fires, agreed that last night's weather report sounded like the monsoon season was about to start and finally got to the point.

"And what brings you all the way down here to Window Rock?"

"I heard on the radio yesterday the FBI's got that Ute Casino robbery all screwed up. You know about that?"

"I'm out of the loop on crimes these days. Don't know anything about it. But it wouldn't be the first time an investigation went sour."

"The radio said they're looking for a damned

airplane," Gershwin said. "None of them fellas could fly anything more complicated than a kite."

Leaphorn raised his eyebrows. This was getting interesting. The last he'd heard, those working the case had absolutely no identifications. But Gershwin had come here to tell him something. He'd let Gershwin talk.

"You want something to drink?" Gershwin waved at the waiter. "Too bad you fellows still have prohibition. Maybe one of those pseudo beers?"

"Coffee'd be good."

The waiter brought it. Leaphorn sipped. Gershwin sampled his milk.

"I knew Cap Stoner," Gershwin said. "They oughta not let them get away with killing him. It's dangerous to have people like that around loose."

Gershwin waited for a response.

Leaphorn nodded.

"'Specially the two younger ones. They're half crazy."

"Sounds like you know them."

"Pretty well."

"You tell the FBI?"

Gershwin studied his milk glass again and found it about half empty. Swirled it. He had a long, narrow face that betrayed his seventy or so years of dry air, windblown sand and dazzling sun, with a mass of wrinkles and sunburn damage. He shifted his bright blue eyes from the milk to Leaphorn.

"There's a problem with that," he said. "I tell the FBI, and sooner or later everybody knows it. Usually sooner. They come up there to see me at the ranch, or they call me. I've got a radio-telephone setup, and you know how that is. Everybody's listening. Worse than the old party line."

Leaphorn nodded. The nearest community to the Gershwin ranch would be Montezuma Creek, or maybe Bluff if his memory served. Not a place where visits from well-dressed FBI agents would go unnoticed, or untalked about.

"You remember that deal in the spring of '98? The feds decided to announce those guys they were looking for are dead. But the folks who snitched on 'em, or helped the cops, they're damn sure keeping their doors locked and their guns loaded and their watchdogs out."

"Didn't the FBI say the gang in 1998 were survivalists? Is it the same people this time?"

Gershwin laughed. "Not if the feds had the names right the last time."

"I'll skip ahead a little," Leaphorn said, "and you tell me if I have it figured right. You want the FBI to catch these guys, but in case they don't, you don't want folks to know you turned them in. So you're going to ask me to pass along the—"

"Whether or not they catch them," Gershwin said. "They have lots of friends."

"The FBI said the 1998 bandits were part of a survivalist organization. Is that what you're saying about these guys?"

"I think they call themselves the Rights Militia. They're for saving the Bill of Rights. Making the Forest Service, and the BLM, and the Park Service people behave so folks can make a living out here."

"You want to give me these names, and I pass them along to the feds. What do I say when the feds ask where I got them?"

Gershwin was grinning at him. "You got it partly wrong," he said. "I've got the names on a piece of paper. I'm going to ask you to give me your word of honor that you'll keep me out of it. If you won't, then I keep the paper. If you promise, and we shake hands on it, then I'll leave the names on the table here and you can pick it up if you want to."

"You think you can trust me?"

"No doubt about it," Gershwin said. "I did before. Remember? And I know some other people who trusted you."

"Why do you want these people caught? Is it just revenge for Cap Stoner?"

"That's part of it," Gershwin said. "But these guys are scary. Some of them anyway. I used to have a little hand in this political stuff with the ones who started it. But then they got too wild."

Gershwin had been about to finish his milk. Now he put the glass down. "Bastards in the Forest Service were acting like they personally owned the mountains," he said. "We lived there all our lives, but now we couldn't graze. Couldn't cut wood. Couldn't hunt elk. And the Land Management bureaucrats were worse. We were the serfs, and they were the lords. We just wanted to have some sort of voice with Congress. Get somebody to remind the bureaucrats who was paying their salaries. Then the crazies moved in. EarthFirst bunch wanting to blow up the bridges the loggers were using. That sort of thing. Then we got some New Age types, and survivalists and Stop World Government people. I sort of phased out."

"So some of these guys did the casino job? Was it political?"

"What I hear, it was supposed to be to finance the cause. But I think some of them needed money to eat," Gershwin said. "If you're not working, I guess you could call that political. But maybe they did want to buy guns and ammunition and explosives. That sort of stuff. Anyway, that's what folks I know in the outfit say. Needed cash to arm themselves to fight off the federal government."

"I wonder how much they got," Leaphorn said.

Gershwin drained his milk. Got up and extracted a folded sheet of paper from his shirt pocket.

"Here it is, Joe. Am I safe to leave it with you? Can you promise you won't turn me in?"

Leaphorn had already thought that through. He could report this conversation to the FBI. They would question Gershwin. He'd deny everything. Nothing accomplished.

"Leave it," Leaphorn said.

Gershwin dropped it on the table, put a dollar beside his milk glass and walked out past the waiter arriving to refill Leaphorn's cup.

Leaphorn took a drink. He picked up the paper and unfolded it. Three names, each followed by a brief description. The first two, Buddy Baker and George Ironhand, meant nothing to him. He stared at the last one. Everett Jorie. That rang a faint and distant bell.

FOUR

CAPTAIN LARGO LOOKED up from the paper he'd been reading, peered over his glasses at Sergeant Chee, and said, "You're a few days early, aren't you? Your calendar break?"

"Captain, you forgot to say, 'Welcome Home. Glad to have you back. Have a seat. Be comfortable.'"

Largo grinned, waved at a chair across from his desk. "I'm almost afraid to ask it, but what makes you so anxious to get back to work?"

Chee sat. "I thought I'd get back to speed gradually. Find out what I've been missing. How'd you get so lucky not to get us dragged into another big manhunt as bush beaters for the federals?"

"That was a relief, that airplane business," Largo said. "On the other hand, you hate to see people shooting policemen and getting away with it. Sets

HUNTING BADGER

another bad example after that summer of '98 fiasco. You want some coffee? Go get yourself a cup, and we'll talk. I want to hear about Alaska after you tell me what you're doing here."

Chee returned with his coffee. He sipped, sat, waited. Largo outwaited him.

"OK," Chee said. "Tell me about the casino robbery. All I know is what I've seen in the papers."

Largo leaned back in his chair, folded his arms across his generous stomach. "Just before four last Saturday morning a pickup drives into the casino lot. Guy gets out, takes out a ladder, climbs up on the roof and cuts the power lines, telephone lines, everything. Another pickup pulls in while this is going on and two guys get out wearing camouflage suits. A Montezuma County deputy, guy named Bai, is standing out there. Then Cap Stoner comes running out, and they shoot both of 'em. You remember Stoner? He used to be a captain with the New Mexico State Police. Worked out of Gallup. Decent man. Then these two guys get into the cashier's room. The money's all sacked up to be handed to the Brinks truck. They make everybody lie down, walk out with the money bags and drive off. Apparently they drove west into Utah because about daylight a Utah Highway Patrolman tries to stop a speeding truck on Route 262 west of Aneth, and they shoot holes in his radiator. Pretty high-powered ammunition according to what Utah tells us."

Largo paused, pushed his bulky frame out of his swivel chair with a grunt. "Need some of my coffee, myself," he said, and headed for the dispenser in the front office.

Sort of good to be back working under Largo, Chee was thinking. Largo had been his boss in his rookie year. Cranky, but he knew his business. Then Largo was coming through the door, holding his cup, talking.

". . . with the lines out, and all the scared gamblers scrambling around trying to get away from the casino, or trying to grab some chips, or whatever you do when the lights go out at the craps table. Anyway, it took a while before anybody knew what the hell was going on and got the word out." Largo eased back into his chair. "I think just about every track you can drive on was blocked by sunup, but by then they had a hell of a lead. Next thing, maybe nine-thirty or so, the word went out somebody in a pickup had shot at the Utah trooper. That shifted the focus westward. The next day a couple of deputy sheriffs found a banged-up pickup abandoned up by the Arizona-Utah border south of Bluff. It fit the description."

"They find any tracks? Were they walking out, changing cars or what?"

"Two sets of tracks around the truck, but here came the feds in their copters"—Largo paused, waved his arms in imitation of helicopter rotors—"and blew everything away."

"Slow learners," Chee said. "That's the same way they fanned away the tracks we'd found across the San Juan in that big thing in '98."

"Maybe we ought to get the Federal Aviation Administration to order all those things grounded during manhunts," Largo said.

"They have anything to match them with? Did they find any tracks at the casino?"

Largo shook his head, paused to sip his coffee, shrugged. "It looked like we were going to have an encore performance of that 1998 business. The federals got a command post set up. Everybody was getting into the act. Regular circus. All we needed was the performing elephants. Had plenty of clowns."

Chee grinned.

"You'd have loved to come home to that."

"I'd have gone right back to Alaska," Chee said. "How'd the FBI find out about the airplane?"

"The owner called in to report it stolen. He said he'd been away up in Denver. When he got home he noticed somebody had broken into his barn, and the airplane he kept there was gone."

"Close to where the pickup was abandoned?"

"Mile and a half or so," Largo said. "Maybe two."

Chee considered that. Largo watched him.

"You're thinking they must have liked to walk."

"Well, there's that," Chee said. "But maybe they wanted to hide the truck. Or if it was found, keep it far enough from the barn so there wouldn't be a connection."

"Uh-huh," Largo said, and sipped coffee. "The FBI says the truck was disabled."

"Out there, it's easy enough to blow tires or bust an oil pan on the rocks if you want to," Chee said.

Largo nodded. "I remember back at Tuba City you did that to a couple of our units, and you claimed you weren't even trying."

Chee let that pass. "Anyway," he said, "I just hope that airplane had enough gas in it to get 'em out of our jurisdiction."

"Full tank, the owner said."

"Makes you think, doesn't it?" Chee said. "I mean how neat everything worked out on both ends of this business."

Largo nodded. "If this was my responsibility now, I'd be getting that rancher's fingerprints and checking out his record and seeing if he was maybe tied up with survivalists, or the Earth Liberation Front, or the tree-huggers, or one of the militia."

"I imagine the FBI is taking care of that. That's the part they're good at," Chee said. "And how about the casino end? What do you hear about that?"

"They think the rent-a-cop was part of the team. Filled 'em in on when the money was sacked up for the Brinks pickup. Which wires to cut, which security people had the evening off. All that."

"Any evidence?"

Largo shrugged. "Nothing much I know about. This Teddy Bai they're holding in the hospital, he had a juvenile record. Witnesses said he was acting skittish all evening. Waiting around out in the lot when he was supposed to be in watching the drunks."

"That's not much," Chee said.

"They probably have more than that," Largo said. "You know how they are. The feds don't tell us locals anything unless they have to. They think we might gossip about it and screw up the investigation."

Chee laughed. "What! Us gossip?"

Largo was grinning, too.

"Have they connected Bai with any of the suspects?"

Largo laughed. "That cold air up in Alaska made an optimist out of you. Not a hint far as I hear. There was some guessing that one of the militia did it to get money for blowing something up, or maybe it was the Earth Liberation Front, but I haven't heard Bai was in any of them. The Earth

Liberation folks have been pretty quiet since they burned up all those buildings at the Vail ski resort. Anyway, if anything checked out, they haven't gotten around to informing the Navajo Tribal Police."

"What do you think, Captain? Has your own grapevine been sending any messages about Bai that you haven't gotten around to telling the feds about?"

Largo studied Chee, his expression suggesting he didn't like the tone of that, and he wasn't sure he would answer it. But he did.

"If Deputy Sheriff Bai is on the wrong side of this one, I haven't heard it," he said.

FIVE

OFFICER BERNADETTE MANUELITO was absolutely correct when she reminded Chee that he knew a lot of people around Shiprock. That had paid off. A chat with a senior San Juan County undersheriff, a drop-in talk with an old friend in the county clerk's office at Aztec, a visit at the Farmington pool hall and another at the Oilmen's Bar and Grill had provided him with a headful of information about the Ute Casino in general and Teddy Bai in particular.

The casino came off better than he'd expected. There was the usual and automatic assumption that organized crime must have a finger in it somehow, but no one could offer any support for that. Otherwise, the people most likely actually to know anything considered it well run. No one had any specific notion about who might have been the robbery's inside man if Bai wasn't. There was agreement that Bai had been a wild kid and mixed opinion on his character in later life, with the consensus in favor of salvation. He had married a girl in the Streams Come Together Clan, but that hadn't lasted. One of the regulars at Oilmen's said since the divorce, Bai came in now and then with a young woman. Who? Chee asked. He didn't know her, but he described her as "cute as a bug's ear." It wasn't the metaphor Chee would have chosen, but it could fit Officer Bernadette Manuelito.

It was also at Oilmen's that he learned Bai had been taking flying lessons.

"Flying lessons?" Chee said. "Really? Where?"

Chee's source for this was a New Mexico State Police dispatcher named Alice Deal. She delayed taking the intended bite from her cheeseburger to wave the free hand toward the Farmington Airport, which sat, like the flight deck of an aircraft carrier, on the mesa looking down on the city.

The sign over the office door of Four Corners Flight declared it the source of charter flights, aircraft rentals, repair, sales, parts, supplies and FAA-certified flight instruction. It didn't appear to be busy in any of those categories when Chee walked into the front office. The only person on the premises was a woman in the manager's office. She interrupted her telephone conversation long enough to wave Chee in.

"Well, now," she was saying, "that's no way to behave. If Betty acts like that, I just wouldn't invite her anymore." She motioned Chee into a chair, listened a moment longer, said, "Well, maybe you're right. I've got a customer. Got to go," and hung up.

Chee introduced himself and his subject.

"Bai," she said. "He owes us for a couple of lessons. The FBI already talked to us about him."

"Could you—"

"Matter of fact, they wanted the names of everybody we'd been teaching from way back. Then they came back again to talk specifically about Teddy."

"Could you tell me if he had his license yet?"

"I doubt it. You're going to have to talk to Jim Edgar," she said. "He's out there talking to the people at the DOE copter, and if he's not there, he'll be working in the hangar."

The copter was a big white Bell with Department of Energy identification markings. Round white bathtub-size containers had been attached above the skids, and a woman in blue coveralls was doing something technical at one of them. The only others present were two men in the same sort of coveralls engaged in conversation. Probably pilot and copilot. Chee tried to guess what the big tubes would contain, with no luck. Obviously none of these people was Jim Edgar.

He found Edgar in the back of the hangar, muttering imprecations and doing something at a workbench to something that looked like a small electric engine. Chee stopped a polite distance away and stood waiting.

Edgar put down a small screwdriver, sucked at a freshly injured thumb and inspected Chee.

Chee explained himself.

"Teddy Bai," Edgar said, inspecting his thumb as he said it. "Well, he'd soloed, but he wasn't near ready to be licensed. He was sort of mediocre as a student. I already told the FBI fellas if he was going to be flying that old L-17, I didn't want to be along on the trip."

"That's the one that was stolen? Why not?"

"He was learning in a new Cessna. Everything modern. Tricycle landing gear. Power-assisted stuff. Different instrumentation. Piper built that L-17 thing for the army in World War Two. Easy enough to fly, I guess, if you understand it, but you'd do a lot of things different than that little Cessna he was learning in."

Edgar paused, seeking a way to explain this. "For example that was one of the first of that sort of plane to use wing flaps. But you can't use 'em on the L-17 if your airspeed is over eighty. And you have to set the tabs on the ground. Little things like that you have to know about."

"And more than fifty years old," Chee said. "Do you know anything about what shape it was in?"

Edgar laughed. "From what I heard on the television, the FBI thinks those casino robbers flew away in it. They better be lucky if they did. Unless Old Man Timms decided to spend some money on it since I saw it."

Chee found himself getting more and more interested in this conversation.

"Was that recently? What was wrong with it?"

Edgar grinned at him. "How much time you got?"

"Any serious stuff?"

"Well, he brought it in for an FAA inspection last autumn. Wanted to get the FAA airworthy certification renewed. Way overdue anyway for an overage plane like that one, and he could have gotten in trouble for just flying it. First thing I noticed he'd let the mice get into it. He keeps it in a barn out at his ranch, which ain't too uncommon out here. But if you do that, you've got to keep the rodents from chewing on things. Set the tail wheel in a bucket of kerosene, maybe. So the wiring and fabric needed inspection, and the engine was running sour. Then these things have twelve-gallon gasoline tanks built into each wing root, feeding into a header tank behind the engine fire wall. Had a little leak in one of the lines."

Edgar shrugged. "Other things, too."

"He got them fixed?"

"He got me to give him an estimate. Said it was way too damn high." Edgar chuckled. "Said he'd sell me the plane for half that. He was going to fly it up to Blanding and get the inspection done at CanyonAire up there. That's the last I saw of him."

"Would you have a phone number for Mr. Timms?" Chee asked. "Or his address?"

"Sure."

Edgar walked across the hangar to his desk and sorted through a Rolodex file. Chee stood watching, trying to understand his motive for what he was doing. What did this have to do with Bernie's boyfriend's problem? Had he spent so many hours fishing and fighting mosquitoes in Alaska that he yearned for some way to get himself into trouble? Was he hungering for some explanation of the wildly illogical way the casino bandits had managed their escape? Whatever his motive, Captain Largo would be very unhappy indeed if Largo learned that Chee had stuck his nose into FBI business and the FBI caught him at it.

Edgar interrupted these thoughts by handing him a copy of a Mountain Mutual Insurance claim form.

"He had me sign off on his insurance claim. He'd left the plane out in the weather and gotten some hail damage," Edgar said. "That was several years ago, but as far as I heard, he hasn't moved."

Chee jotted the information he wanted into his notebook, thanked Edgar and headed back to his truck. Then a sudden thought caused him to grin. With the plane now stolen, Timms would be filing another insurance claim.

"Mr. Edgar," he shouted. "Do you remember what you'd have had to charge Timms for those repairs? When he said he'd sell it for half your estimate?"

"I think the estimate was close to four thousand dollars," Edgar said. "But if I was stupid enough to want that thing, and made him an offer, he'd have said it was a valuable antique and asked for about thirty thousand."

Chee laughed. That, he thought, would probably be about what Timms would claim from his insurance company.

"How about using your telephone?" Chee asked. "And the directory."

He punched in the Mountain Mutual Insurance Farmington agent's number, identified himself, asked the woman who ran the place if she still handled Eldon Timms's insurance.

"Unfortunately," she said.

"His airplane, too?"

"Same answer," she said. "Or I guess you'd say the former airplane, the one those robbers stole?"

"Does he have another one?"

"Lordy, I hope not," she said.

"He file a claim on it?"

"Yes, indeedy, he did. Right away. I just heard about the robbers stealing a plane out there and flying off in it, and he's on the phone asking about getting his money. And I said, 'What's the hurry. They have to land someplace and the cops recover it and you get it back.' And he said, 'If that happens, we tear up the claim.'"

"How much was the insurance?"

"Forty thousand," she said. "He just jacked it up to that a couple of months ago."

"Sounds like quite a bit for a fifty-year-old aircraft," Chee said.

"I thought so," she said. "But no skin off my nose. Timms was the one paying the premium. He said it was an antique, a real rare airplane, and he was going to sell it to that military-aircraft museum in Tucson. I have a feeling he was using that higher insured value to sort of—you know—establish a sales price."

Edgar had been standing nearby, listening.

"That do it for you?"

"Yeah," Chee said, "and thanks. But by the way, what's that Energy Department helicopter doing here? And what's the DOE doing with those big white pods?"

"Actually, the pods aren't DOE, they're EPA," Edgar said. "You are looking at a rare case of inter-agency cooperation. The Environmental Protection bunch borrows the copter and the pilots from the DOE's Nevada test site. They got radiation detectors in those pods, and they use them to find old uranium mines. Get the hot stuff covered up."

After he left Four Corners Flight, Chee dropped in at the New Mexico State Police office below the airport and made two more calls—the first one to the Air War Museum at Tucson. Yes, the manager told him, Mr. Timms had flown his L-17 down in June and offered it for sale. And, yes, they would have liked to add it to their collection, but they hadn't made an offer. Why not? The usual reason, said the manager. He wanted way too much for it. He was asking fifty thousand.

The second call was to Cowboy Dashee, his old friend from boyhood. But it wasn't just to reminisce. Deputy Sheriff Dashee worked for the Sheriff's Department of Apache County, Arizona, which meant the ranch of Eldon Timms—at least the south end of it—might be in Deputy Dashee's jurisdiction.

SIX

FOR NO REASON except habit born of childhood in a crowded hogan, Joe Leaphorn awoke with the first light of dawn. The bedroom he and Emma had shared for three happy decades faced both the sunrise and the noisy street. When Leaphorn had noted the noise disadvantage to Emma she had pointed out that the quieter bedroom had no windows facing the dawn. No further explanation was needed.

Emma was a true Navajo traditional with the traditional's need to greet the new day. That was one of the countless reasons Leaphorn loved her. Besides, while Leaphorn was no longer truly a traditional, no longer offered a pinch of pollen to the rising sun, he still treasured the old ways of his people.

This morning, however, he had a good reason

for sleeping late. Professor Louisa Bourebonette was sleeping in the quieter bedroom, and Leaphorn didn't want to awaken her. So he lay under the sheet, watched the eastern horizon turn flame red, listened to the automatic coffeemaker go to work in the kitchen, and considered what the devil to do with the names Gershwin had given him. The three had stolen themselves an airplane and flown away, which took some of the pressure off. Still, if Gershwin was right, having their identities would certainly be useful to those trying to catch them.

Leaphorn yawned, stretched, smelled coffee, wondered if he could get to the kitchen and pour a cup quietly enough not to disturb Louisa. Wondered, too, what solution she would offer for his dilemma if he presented it to her. Emma would have told him to forget it. Locking robbers in prison helped no one, she'd say. They should be cured of the disharmony that was causing this bad behavior. Prison didn't accomplish that. A Mountain Way ceremony, with all their friends and relatives gathered to support them, would drive the dark wind out of them and restore them to *hozho*.

A clatter in the kitchen interrupted that thought. Leaphorn jumped out of bed and put on his bathrobe. He found Louisa standing at the stove, fully dressed and cooking pancakes.

"I'm using your mix," she said. "They'd be a lot better if you had some buttermilk."

Leaphorn rescued his mug from the sink, rinsed it, poured himself a cup, and sat by the table watching Louisa, remembering the ten thousand mornings he had watched Emma from the same chair. Emma was shorter, slimmer, and always wore skirts. Louisa had on jeans and a flannel shirt. Her hair was short and gray. Emma's was long and a luminous black. That hair was her only source of vanity. Emma had hated to have it cut even for the brain surgery that killed her.

"You're up early," Leaphorn said.

"Blame it on your culture," Louisa said. "These old-timers I need to talk to have been up an hour already. They'll be in bed by sundown."

"How about your translator? Did you ever manage to get hold of him?"

"I'll try again after breakfast," Louisa said. "Young people have more normal sleeping habits."

They ate pancakes.

"Something's on your mind," Louisa said. "Right?"

"Why do you say that?"

"Because it's true," Louisa said. "I could tell last night when we were having dinner down at the Inn. Couple of times you started to say something, but you didn't."

True enough. And why hadn't he? Because it

would have taken him too close to his relationship with Emma—this hashing over of something he was working on. But now in the light of morning he saw nothing wrong with it. He told Louisa about Gershwin, the three names and his promise—ambiguous and vague.

"Did you shake hands on it? Any of that male-chivalry stuff?"

Leaphorn grinned. Louisa's way of striking right to the heart of matters was something he liked about her.

"Well, we shook hands, but it was sort of a 'good-bye, glad to see you again' handshake. No cutting our wrists and mixing blood," he said. "He had the identification information written on a piece of paper, and he just left that on the table. With sort of an unspoken understanding that if I took it, I could do whatever I wanted with it. But promising him confidentiality was implied no matter what I did."

"And you took the paper?"

"Not exactly. I read it, then wadded it up and dropped it in the wastebasket."

She was smiling at him, shaking her head.

"You're right," he said. "Throwing it away didn't work. I'm still stuck with the promise."

She nodded, cleared her throat, sat very straight. "Mr. Leaphorn," she said, "I remind you that you are under oath to tell this grand jury the truth and the whole truth. How did you obtain this information?" Louisa stared over her glasses at him, her stern look. "Then you say you read it off a piece of paper left on a restaurant table, and the lawyer asks if you know who left the paper, and . . ."

Leaphorn raised his hand. "I know," he said.

"Two choices, really. After all, that Gershwin jerk was just trying to use you. You could just forget it. Or you could figure out some sneaky way to get the names to the FBI. How about an anonymous letter? In fact, don't you wonder why he didn't write one himself?"

"I guess it was timing. A couple of days pass before the letter gets delivered. Then if it's anonymous, it goes right to the bottom of the pile," Leaphorn said. "I guess he knew that. I think he's afraid these days. That the bandits know that he knows, and they don't trust him, and if they aren't caught, they'll be coming after him."

Louisa laughed. "I'd say they have pretty good reason not to trust him. You shouldn't, either."

"I thought about faxing it in from some commercial place where nobody knows me, or sending an e-mail. But just about everything is traceable these days. And now there's a reward out, so they'll be getting dozens of tips by now. Probably hundreds."

"I guess so," Louisa said. "Why don't you call one of your old FBI buddies? Do the same thing to them Gershwin's doing to you?"

Leaphorn laughed. "I tried that. I called Jay Kennedy. You remember me telling you about him? Used to be Agent in Charge at Gallup, and we worked on several things together. Anyway, he's retired over in Durango. So I tried it on him. No luck."

"What did he say?"

"Same thing you just told me. If he passes it along to the Bureau, they ask him where he got it. He tells 'em me. They ask me where I got it."

"So what's your solution? How about disguising your voice and giving them a telephone call?"

"I might try that. The FBI has them flying away. I could tell them one of the guys is a pilot. That would be easy for them to check, and if one of them happens to be a flier, then they'd be interested. But that's just half the problem." He paused to take another bite of pancake.

She watched him chew, waited, sighed. Said, "OK, what's the other half?"

"Maybe these three guys had nothing to do with it. Maybe Gershwin just wants them hassled for some personal reason, and if the robbers aren't caught, this would damn sure do that sooner or later."

She nodded. "I'll take it under advisement, then," she said, and left the kitchen to call her interpreter.

By the time Leaphorn had the dishes washed she was back, looking disheartened.

"Not only is he sick, he has laryngitis. He can hardly talk. I guess I'll head back to Flagstaff and try it later."

"Too bad," Leaphorn said.

"Another thing. He'd told them we were coming today. And no telephone, of course, to tell them we're not."

"Where do these guys live?"

Louisa's expression brightened. "Are you about to volunteer to interpret? The Navajo's a fellow named Dalton Cayodito and the address I have is Red Mesa Chapter House. The other one's a Ute. Lives at Towaoc on the Ute Mountain Reservation. How's your Ute?"

"Maybe fifty words or so," Leaphorn said. "But I could help you with Cayodito."

"Let's do it," Louisa said.

"I'm thinking that a couple of the men on that list are supposed to live up there in that border country. One of 'em's Casa Del Eco Mesa. That couldn't be too far from the chapter house."

Louisa laughed. "Mixing business with pleasure. Or I should say your business with my business. Or maybe my business with something that really isn't your business."

"The one who has a place up there—according to the notes on that paper anyway—is Everett Jorie. I can't place him but the name's familiar. Probably something out of the distant past. I thought we could ask around."

Louisa was smiling at him. "You've forgotten you're retired," she said. "For a minute there, I thought you were going along for the pleasure of my company."

Leaphorn drove the first lap—the 110 miles from his house to the Mexican Water Trading Post. They stopped there for a sandwich and to learn if anyone there knew how to find Dalton Cayodito. The teenage Navajo handling the cash register did.

"An old, old man," she said. "Did he used to be a singer? If that's him, he did the Yeibichai sing for my grandmother. Is that the one you're looking for?"

Louisa said it was. "We heard he lived up by the Red Mesa Chapter House."

"He lives with his daughter," the girl said. "That's Madeleine Horsekeeper, I think they call her. Her place is—" She paused, thought, made a gesture of frustration with her hands, penciled a map on a grocery sack and handed it to Louisa.

"How about a man named Everett Jorie?" Leaphorn said. "You know where to find him? Or Buddy Baker? Or George Ironhand."

She didn't, but the man who had been stacking

Spam cans on shelves along the back wall thought he could help.

"Hey," he said. "Joe Leaphorn. I thought you'd retired. What you want Jorie for? If you got a law against being a damned nuisance, you oughta had him locked up long ago."

They left the trading post a quarter hour later armed with explicit instructions on how to find the two places Jorie might be located, an addendum to the grocery-sack map outlining which turns to take from which roads to find Ironhand, and a vague notion that Baker might have moved into Blanding. Along with that they took a wealth of speculative gossip about Utah-Arizona border-land political ambitions, social activities, speculation about who might have robbed the Ute Casino, an account of the most recent outrages committed by the Forest Service, Bureau of Land Management, Bureau of Reclamation, Park Service, and other federal, state and county agencies against the well-being of various folks who lived their hardscrabble lives along the Utah border canyon country.

"No wonder the militia nuts can sign people up," Louisa said, as they drove away. "Is it as bad as that?"

"They're mostly just trying to enforce unpopular laws," Leaphorn said. "Mostly fine people. Now and then somebody gets arrogant."

"OK, now," Louisa said. "These guys you mentioned in there—Jorie and Ironhand and so forth. I guess they're the three who robbed the casino?"

"Or maybe robbed it," Leaphorn said. "If we believe Gershwin."

Louisa was driving and spent a few moments looking thoughtful.

"You know," she said, "as long as I've been out here I still can't get used to how everybody knows everybody."

"You mean that guy at the store recognizing me? I was a cop out here for years."

"But living where? About a hundred and fifty miles away. But I didn't mean just you. The cashier knew all about Everett Jorie. And people know about Baker and Ironhand living"—she waved an expressive hand at the window—"living way the hell out there someplace. Where I came from people didn't even know who lived three houses down the block."

"Lot more people in Baltimore," Leaphorn said.

"Not a lot more people on our block."

"More people in your block, I'll bet, than in a twenty-mile circle around here," Leaphorn said. He was remembering the times he'd spent in Washington, in New York, in Los Angeles, when he'd considered this difference between urban and rural social attitudes.

"I have a theory not yet endorsed by any

sociologist," he said. "You city folks have so many people crowding you they're a bother. So you try to avoid them. We rural people don't have enough, so we're interested. We sort of collect them."

"You'll have to make it a lot more complicated than that to get the sociologists to adopt it," Louisa said. "But I know what you're driving at."

"Out here, everybody looks at you," he said. "You're somebody different. Hey, here's another human, and I don't even know him yet. In the city, nobody wants to make eye contact. They have built themselves a little privacy bubble—hard to get any privacy in crowded places—and if you look at them, or speak on the street, then you're an intruder."

Louisa looked away from the road to give him a sidewise grin.

"I take it you don't care for the busy, exciting, stimulating city life," she said. "I've also heard it put another way. Like 'rural folks tend to be nosy busybodies.'"

They were still discussing that when they turned off the pavement of U.S. 160 onto the dirt road that climbed over the Utah border onto the empty, broken highlands of the Casa Del Eco Mesa. She slowed while Leaphorn checked the map against the landscape. The clouds were climbing on the western horizon, and the outriders of the front were speckling the landscape spreading away to the west with a crazy-quilt pattern of shadows.

"If my memory's good, we hit an intersection up here about seven miles," he said. "Take the bad road to the right, and it takes you to the Red Mesa Chapter House. Take the worse road to the left, and it gets you to Highway 191 and on to Bluff."

"There's the junction up ahead," she said. "We do a left? Right?"

"Left is right," Leaphorn said. "And after the turn, we're looking for a track off to our right."

They found it, and a dusty, bumpy mile later, they came to the place of Madeleine Horsekeeper, which was a fairly new double-wide mobile home, with an attendant hogan of stacked stones, sheep pens, outhouse, brush arbor and two parked vehicles—an old pickup truck and a new blue Buick Regal. Madeleine Horsekeeper was standing in the doorway greeting them, with a stern-looking fortyish woman standing beside her. She proved to be Horsekeeper's daughter, who taught social studies at Grey Hills High in Tuba City. She would sit in on the interview with Hosteen Cayodito, her maternal grandfather, and would make sure the interpreting was accurate. Or do it herself.

Which was fine with Joe Leaphorn. He had thought of a way to spend the rest of this day that would be much more interesting than listening for modifications and evolutions in the legends he'd grown up with. That talk with Louisa about how folks in lonely country knew everything about their neighbors had reminded him of Under-sheriff Oliver Potts, now retired. If anyone knew the three on Gershwin's list, it would be Oliver.

SEVEN

OLIVER POTTS'S MODEST stone residence was shaded by a grove of cottonwoods beside Recapture Creek, maybe five miles northeast of Bluff and a mile down a rocky road even worse than described at the Chevron station where Leaphorn had topped off his gas tank.

"Yes," said the middle-aged Navajo woman who answered his knock, "Ollie's in there resting his eyes." She laughed. "Or he's supposed to be, anyway. Actually he's probably reading, or studying one of his soap operas." She ushered Leaphorn into the living room, said, "Ollie, here's company," and disappeared.

Potts looked up from the television, examined Leaphorn through thick-lensed glasses. "Be damned. You look like Joe Leaphorn, but if it is, you're out of uniform."

"I've been out of uniform almost as long as you have," Leaphorn said, "but not long enough to watch the soap operas."

He took the chair Potts offered. They exhausted the social formalities, agreed retirement became tiresome after the first couple of months, and reached the pause that said it was time for business. Leaphorn recited Gershwin's three names. Could Potts tell him anything about them?

Potts hadn't seemed to be listening. He had laid himself back in his recliner chair, glasses off now and eyes almost closed, either dozing or thinking about it. After a moment he said, "Odd mix you got there. What kind of mischief have those fellows been up to?"

"Probably nothing," Leaphorn said. "I'm just checking on some gossip."

It took Potts a moment to accept that. His eyes remained closed, but a twist of his lips expressed skepticism. He nodded. "Actually, Ironhand and Baker fit well enough. We've had both of them in a time or two. Nothing serious that we could make stick. Simple assault, I think it was, on Baker, and a DWI and resisting arrest. George Ironhand, he's a little meaner. If I remember right, it was assault with a deadly weapon, but he got off. And then we had him as a suspect one autumn butchering time in a little business about whose steers he was cutting up into steaks and stew beef."

He produced a faint smile, reminiscing. "Turned out to be an honest mistake, if you know what I mean. And then, the feds got interested in him. Somebody prodded them into doing something about that protected antiquities law. They had the idea that his little bitty ranch was producing way too many of those old pots and the other Anasazi stuff he was selling. They couldn't find no ruins on his place, and the feds figured he was climbing over the fence and digging them out of sites on federal land."

"I remember that now," Leaphorn said. "Nothing came of it? Right?"

"Usual outcome. Case got dropped for lack of evidence."

"You said they fit better than Jorie. Why's that?"

"Well, they're both local fellas. Ironhand's a Ute and Baker's born in the county. Both rode in the rodeo a little, as I remember. Worked here and there. Probably didn't finish high school. Sort of young." He grinned at Leaphorn. "By our standards, anyway. Thirty or forty. I think Baker is married. Or was."

"They buddies?"

That produced another thoughtful silence. Then: "I think they both worked for El Paso Natural once, or one of the pipeline outfits. If it's important, I can tell you who to ask. And then I think both of them were into that militia outfit. Minutemen I think they called it."

Potts opened his eyes now, squinted, rubbed his hand across them, restored the glasses and looked at Leaphorn. "You heard of our militia?"

"Yeah," Leaphorn said. "They had an organizing meeting down at Shiprock last winter."

"You sign up?"

"Dues were too high," Leaphorn said. "But they seemed to be getting some recruits."

"We got a couple of versions up here. Militia to protect us from the Bureau of Land Management and the Forest Service and the seventy-two other federal agencies. Then the survivalists, getting us ready for when all those black helicopters swarm in to round us up for the United Nations concentration camps. And then for the rich kids, we have our Save Our Mountains outfit trying to fix it so the Ivy Leaguers don't have to associate with us redneck working folks when they want to get away from their tennis courts."

Potts had his eyes closed again. Leaphorn waited, Navajo fashion, until he was sure Potts had finished this speech. He hadn't.

"Come to think of it," Potts added, "maybe that's how you could tie in ole Everett Jorie. He used to be one of the militia bunch."

Potts sat up. "Remember? He used to run that afternoon talk show on one of the Durango radio stations. Right-winger. Sort of an intellectual version of what's his name? That fat guy. Ditto Head. Made him sound almost sane. Anyway, Jorie was always promoting the militia. He'd quote Plato and Shakespeare and read passages from Thoreau and Thomas Paine to do it. Finally got so wild the station fired him. I think he was a fairly big shot in the militia. I heard Baker was a member. At least I'd see him at meetings. I think I saw George at one, too."

"Jorie still in the militia?"

"I don't think so," Potts said. "Heard they had a big falling-out. It's all hearsay, of course, but the gossip was he wanted 'em to do less talking and writing to their congressman and things like that and get more dramatic."

Potts had his eyes wide open now, peering at Leaphorn, awaiting the question.

"Like what?"

"Just gossip, you know. But like blowing up a Forest Service office."

"Or maybe a dam?"

Potts chuckled. "You're thinking of that big manhunt a while back. When the guys stole the water truck and shot the policeman, and the FBI decided they were going to fill the truck with explosives, blow up the dam and drain Lake Mead."

"What's your theory on that one?"

"Stealing the water truck? I figured they needed it to water their marijuana crop."

Leaphorn nodded.

"FBI didn't buy that. I guess there was budget hearings coming up. They needed some terrorism to talk about, and if it's just pot farmers at work, that hands the ball to the Drug Enforcement folks. The competition. The enemy."

"Yeah," Leaphorn said.

"Now," Potts said, "it is time for you to tell me what you're up to. I heard you been working as a private investigator. Did the Ute Casino people sign you up to get their money back?"

"No," Leaphorn said. "Tell the truth I don't know what I'm up to myself. Just heard something, and had time on my hands, and got to wondering about it, so I thought I'd ask around."

"Just bored then," Potts said, sounding as if he didn't believe it. "Nothing interesting on TV, so you thought you'd just take a three-hour drive up here to Utah and do some visiting. Is that it?"

"That's close enough," Leaphorn said. "And I've got one more name to ask about. You know Roy Gershwin?"

"Everybody knows Roy Gershwin. What's he up to?"

"Is there anything to connect him to the other three?"

Potts thought about it. "I don't know why I want to tell you anything, Joe, when you won't tell me why you're askin'. But let's see. He used to show up at militia meetings a while back. He was fighting with the BLM, and the Forest Service, and the Soil Conservation Service, or whatever they call it now, over a grazing lease and over a timber-cutting permit, too, I think it was. That had gotten him into an antigovernment mood. I think Baker used to work for him once on that ranch he runs. And I think his place runs up against Jorie's, so that makes them neighbors."

"Good neighbors?"

Potts restored his glasses, sat up and looked at Leaphorn. "Don't you remember Gershwin? He wasn't the kind of fellow you were good neighbors with. And Jorie's even worse. As a matter of fact, I think Jorie was suing Roy over something or other. Suing people was one of Jorie's hobbies."

"About what?"

Potts shrugged. "This and that. He sued me once 'cause his livestock was running on my place, and I penned them up, and he wanted to take 'em back without paying me for my feed. With Gershwin, I don't remember. I think they were fighting over the boundaries of a grazing lease." He paused, considering. "Or maybe it was locking a gate on an access road."

"Were any of those three people pilots?"

"Fly airplanes?" Potts was grinning. "Like rob the Ute Casino and then stealing Old Man Timms's airplane to fly away? I thought you was retired from being a cop."

Leaphorn could think of no response to that.

"You think maybe those three guys did it?" Potts said. "Well, that's as good a guess as I could make. Why not? You have any idea where they'd fly to?"

"No ideas about anything much," Leaphorn said. "I'm just idling away some time."

"Several ranchers around here have their little planes," Potts said. "None of those guys, though. I remember hearing Jorie going on about flying for the navy on his talk show, but I know he didn't have a plane. And airplanes was one of the things Ironhand used to bitch about. People flying over his ranch. Said they scared his livestock. He thought it was people spying on him when he was stealing pots. Baker and Ironhand now. Far as I know, neither of them ever had anything better than a used pickup."

"You know where Jorie lives?" Leaphorn asked.

Potts stared at him. "You going to go see him? What you going to say? Did you rob the casino? Shoot the cops?"

"If he did, he won't be home. Remember? He flew away."

"Oh, right," Potts said, and laughed. "If the Federal Bureau of Ineptitude says it, it must be true." He pushed himself up. "Let me get myself a piece of paper and my pencil. I'll draw you a little map."

EIGHT

COWBOY DASHEE ROLLED down the window of Apache County Sheriff's Department Patrol Unit 4 as Chee walked up. He leaned out, staring at Chee.

"The cooler's in the trunk," Dashee said. "Dry ice in it, with room enough for about forty pounds of smoked Alaska salmon caught by my Navajo friend. But where's the damned fish?"

"I hate to tell you about that," Chee said. "The girls had this big welcome-home salmonfest for me at Shiprock. Dancing around the campfire down by the San Juan, swimming bareback in the river. Just me and nine of those pretty teachers from the community college." Chee opened the passenger-side door and slid in. "I should have remembered to invite you."

"You should have," Dashee said. "Since you're

going to work me for some favor. From what you said on the telephone, you're going to try to get me in trouble with the FBI. What do you want me to do?"

They'd met at the Lukachukai Chapter House, Chee making the long drive from Farmington over the Chuska Mountains and Dashee up from his station at Chinle. Dashee arrived a little late. And now was accused by Chee of being corrupted from his stern Hopi ways and learning how to operate on "Navajo Time," which recognized neither late nor early. They wasted a few minutes exchanging barbs and grinning at one another as old friends do, before Chee answered Dashee's question.

"What I'd like you to do is help me get straightened out on that business with the stolen airplane," Chee said.

"Eldon Timms's airplane? What's to straighten out? The bandidos stole it and flew away. And thank God for that." Dashee made a wry face. "If you see it anywhere, just call the nearest office of the Federal Bureau of Investigation."

"You think that's what actually happened?"

Dashee laughed. "Let's just say I hope the feds got it right this time. Otherwise, we both ought to apply for a leave. I don't think I could stand a repeat of that Great Four Corners Manhunt of 1998. You want to go crashing around in the canyons again?"

"I could get along without that," Chee said, and told Dashee what he'd learned about the Timms L-17, and the insurance, and Timms's futile effort to sell it, and all the rest. "You mind us driving over there and showing me where the pickup was found, and the barn where Timms kept the plane? Just going over that part of it with me?"

Dashee studied him. "You're wanting to use your old buddy Cowboy because you're not back on duty yet, and don't have any business out there anyway even if you were. And me, being a deputy sheriff of Apache County, Arizona, could claim I had some legitimate reason to be butting in on a case the FBI has taken over. So if the feds get huffy about us nosy locals, they can blame me. Am I right?"

"That's about it," Chee said. "Does it make sense to you?"

Dashee snorted, started the engine. "Well, then, let's go. Let's get there while we still have a little daylight."

The sun was low when Dashee stopped the patrol car. The ragged top of Comb Ridge to the west was producing a zigzag pattern of light and shadow across the sagebrush flats of the Nokaito Bench. The Gothic Creek bottoms below were already a crooked streak of darkness. Dashee was pointing down into the canyon. "Down there but for the grace of God and Timms's convenient airplane go you and I," he said. "Once again testing the federal law-enforcement theory that to locate fugitives you send out local cops until the perps start shooting them, thereby giving away their location."

"It used to work in India when the nabobs were hunting tigers," Chee said. "Only they did it with beaters instead of deputy sheriffs. They'd send those guys in to provoke the animals."

"I thought they used goats."

"That was later," Chee said. "After the beaters joined the union. Now why not tell me why we're stopping here."

"High ground. You can see the lay of the land from here." Dashee pointed northeast. "Up there, maybe three miles, is the Timms place. You can't see it because it's beyond that ridge, down a slope." He pointed again. "This road we're on angles along the rim of the mesa over Gothic Creek, then swings back past the Timms place, and then sort of peters out at a widow woman's ranch up toward the San Juan. That's the end of it. The truck was abandoned about a mile and a half up ahead."

Chee hoisted himself onto the front fender. "All I know about this case is what I've heard since I got home. Fill me in. What's the official Theory of the Crime?"

Dashee grinned. "You think the feds would tell an Apache County deputy?"

"No. But somebody in the Denver FBI, or maybe the Salt Lake office, or Phoenix, or Albuquerque, fills in some state-level cop, and he tells somebody else, and the word spreads and pretty soon somebody else tells your sheriff, and—" Chee made an all-encompassing gesture. "So everybody knows in about three hours, and the federals maintain their deniability."

"OK," Dashee said. "What we hear goes like this. This Teddy Bai fella, the one the FBI is holding at the Farmington hospital, he tells some of the wrong people how easy it would be to rob the Ute Casino, and the word gets back to some medium-level hoods. Maybe Las Vegas hoods, maybe Los Angeles. I've heard it both ways, and it's just guesswork. Anyway, the theory is Bai gets contacted. He's offered a slice if he'll help with the details, like getting the timing just right, all the inside stuff they need to know. Who's on guard when. When the bank truck comes. How to cut off the power, telephones, so forth. Bai is a flier, he tells them that Timms has this old army short-takeoff recon airplane they can grab for the getaway. He'll fly it for them. But they know that Bai's local. He'll be missed. He'll be the way the hoods planning this can be traced. So they bring along their own pilot, shoot Bai, drive out to the Timms place, tear up the pickup truck so the cops will think they had to abandon it out here, steal the plane and"—Dashee flapped his arms—"away they go."

Chee nodded.

"You're thinking about Timms," Dashee said. "The theory is they planned to kill him, too. That would have given them more time. But he wasn't home. On his way home Timms heard about the robbery on the news and then found the lock on his barn busted, and his airplane gone, and he notified the cops. And since we're closest, we got sent to check it out."

Chee nodded again.

"You don't like that, either?"

"I'm just thinking," Chee said. "Show me where they left the truck."

Doing that took them into the rugged, stony treeless territory where no one except surveyors seems to know exactly where Arizona ends and Utah begins. It involved a descent on a bad dirt road from the mesa top and took them past a flat expanse of drought-dwarfed sage where a white tanker truck was parked with its door open and a man sitting in the front seat reading something.

Dashee waved at him. "Rosie Rosner," Dashee said. "Claims he has the easiest job in North America. Even easier than being a deputy. Three or four times a day an Environmental Protection Agency copter flies in here, he refuels it, and then nods off again until it comes back."

"I think I saw that copter at the Farmington Airport," Chee said. "Guy there said they're locating abandoned uranium mines. Looking for radioactive dumps."

"I asked the guy if he'd seen our bandidos driving in," Dashee said. "But no such luck. They started doing this the next day."

Dashee honked at the driver and waved. "Come to think of it, I guess the timing was pretty lucky for him."

About a mile beyond the refueling truck Dashee stopped again and got out.

"Take a look at this." He pointed to a black outcrop of basalt beside the track, partly hidden by an outstretched limb of a four-wing saltbush and a collection of tumbleweeds.

"Here's where they banged up their oil pan on the truck," he said. "Either they didn't know the road, or they weren't paying attention or they swerved just a little bit to do it on purpose."

"So we'd think they abandoned the truck because they didn't have any choice," Chee said.

"Maybe. You'd see they didn't drive it much farther."

After another few hundred yards Dashee turned off the packed earth of the unimproved road into an even vaguer track. He rolled the patrol car down a slope into a place where humps of blown sand supported a growth of Mormon tea and a few scraggly junipers.

"Here we are," he said. "I'm parking just about exactly where they left the pickup."

Chee climbed one of the mounds, looked down at the place the truck had been and all around.

"Could you see the truck from the track? Just driving past?"

"If you knew where to look," Dashee said. "And Timms would have noticed the oil leak, and the tracks turning off. He would have been looking."

"You find any tracks?"

"Sure," Dashee said. "Both sides of the truck where they got out. Two sets. Then somebody told the feds, and here comes the copters full of the city boys in their bulletproof suits."

"The copters blew away the tracks?"

Dashee nodded. "Just like they did it for us in the '98 business. When I called it in, I asked 'em to warn the feds about that." Dashee laughed. "They said that'd be like trying to tell the pope how to hear confessions. Anyway, the light wasn't too bad, and I took a roll of photographs. Boot prints and the places they put stuff they unloaded."

"Like what?"

"Mark left by a rifle butt. Something that

might have been a box. Big sack. So forth." Da-shee shrugged.

Chee laughed. "Like a sack full of Ute Casino money, maybe. By the way, how much did they get?"

"An 'undetermined amount,' according to the FBI. But the unofficial and approximate estimate I hear was four hundred and eighty-six thousand, nine hundred and eleven dollars."

Chee whistled.

"All unmarked money, of course," Dashee added. "And lots of pockets full of big-value chips which honest folks grabbed off the roulette tables while escaping in the darkness."

"Did the tracks head right off toward the Timms place? Or where?"

"We didn't have much time to look. The sheriff called right back and said the FBI wanted us not to mess around the scene. Just back off and guard the place."

"Not much time to look, huh?" Chee said. "What did you see when you did look? What was in the truck?"

"Nothing much. They'd stolen it off of one of those Mobil Oil pump jack sites, and it had some of those greasy wrenches, wipe rags, empty beer cans, hamburger wrappers, so forth. Stuff left under the seats and on the floorboards. Girlie maga-zine in a door side pocket, receipts for some gas purchases." Dashee shrugged. "About what you'd expect."

"Anything in the truck bed?"

"We thought we had something there," Dashee said. "A good-as-new-looking transistor radio there on the truck bed. Looked expensive, too." He shrugged. "But it was broken."

"Broken. It wouldn't play?"

"Not a sound," Dashee said. "Maybe the battery was down. Maybe it broke when whoever threw it back there."

"More likely they threw it back there because it was already broken," Chee said. He was staring westward, down into the wash, and past it into the broken Utah border country, the labyrinth of canyons and mesa where the Navajo Tribal Police, and police from a score of other state, federal and county agencies had searched for the killers in the '98 manhunt.

"You know, Cowboy," Chee said, "I've got a feeling we're a little bit north of your jurisdiction here. I think Apache County and Arizona stopped a mile or two back there and we're in Utah."

"Who cares?" Dashee said. "What's more interesting is you can't see the Timms place from here. It's maybe a mile down the track."

"Let's go take a look," Chee said.

It was, judging by the police car odometer, 1.3 miles. The road wandered down a slope into a

TONY HILLERMAN

sagebrush flat, to a pitched-roof stone house and a cluster of outbuildings. A plank barn with a red tar-paper roof dominated the scene. From a pole jutting above it a white wind sock dangled, awaiting a breeze to return it to duty. Chee noticed an east–west strip of the flat had been graded clear of brush. He also noticed that the road continued beyond this place, reduced to a set of parallel ruts and wandering across the flat to disappear over a ridge.

Chee pointed. "Where's it go?"

"Another three, four miles, there's another little ranch, the widow I told you about," Dashee said. "It dead-ends there."

"No outlet then? Back to the highway?"

"Unless you can fly," Dashee said.

"I had been thinking that maybe the perps had turned off on this road figuring they'd circle past a roadblock on U.S. 191 up toward Bluff. I guess that would mean they didn't know this country."

"Yeah," Dashee said, "I thought about that. The feds figured it means they knew the Timms airplane was there waiting for them."

"Or they knew a trail down into Gothic Canyon, and down that to the San Juan, and down the river to some other canyon."

"Oh, man," Dashee said. "Don't even think of that." And he pulled the car into Eldon Timms's dusty yard.

A woman was standing on the shady side of the house watching them. Wearing jeans, well-worn boots, a man's shirt with the sleeves rolled and a wide-brimmed straw hat. About middle seventies, Chee guessed. But maybe a little younger. Whites didn't have the skin to deal with this dry sunshine. They wrinkled up about ten years early. She was walking toward the car as Chee and Dashee got out, squinting at them.

"That's Eleanor Ashby," Dashee said. "Widow living over the hill there. She looks after Timms's livestock when he's away. She said they trade off."

"Sheriff," Eleanor Ashby said, "what brings you back over here? You forget something?"

"We were looking for Mr. Timms," Dashee said, and introduced Chee and himself. "I forgot some things I wanted to ask him."

"You needed to go to Blanding to do that," she said. "He headed up there this morning to talk to the insurance people."

"Well, it's nothing important. Just some details I needed to fill in for the paperwork. I forgot to ask him what time of day it was he got back here and found his airplane was missing. But it can wait. I'll catch him next time I get back up this way."

"Maybe I can help you with that," Eleanor said. "Let me think just for a minute, and I can get close to it. He was supposed to bring me some stuff from Blanding, and I thought I'd heard an airplane, so I came on over. Thinking he'd gotten home, but he wasn't back yet."

"About noon?" Chee asked. "You're lucky you weren't here when the bandits were."

"Don't I know it," Eleanor said. "They just might have shot me. Or taken me as a hostage. God knows what. Still scares me when I think about it."

"That plane you heard. You think that was the bandits flying off in Mr. Timms's airplane?"

"No. I just figured Timms had flown over to take a look, and then went on over to the other little place he has over by Mexican Water."

Chee looked at Dashee and found Dashee looking at him.

"Wait a minute," Dashee said. "You mean Timms had flown the plane up to Blanding?"

Eleanor laughed. "Course not," she said. "But that's what I was thinking. Sometimes he took the plane, if he could land where he was going. Sometimes he took his truck."

"But the plane was here when you came by at noon?" Chee asked.

She nodded. "Yeah. Locked in the barn."

"You saw it in there?"

"I saw that big old lock he uses on the door hasp." She chuckled. "You lock that old airplane in there, it can't get out."

"You didn't see his truck?" Chee asked.

"It wasn't here. He—" She frowned at Chee. "What do you mean? What are you thinking?"

"Does he just leave his truck out front?" Dashee asked. "Or somewhere you could have seen it?"

"He keeps it in that shed behind the house," Mrs. Eleanor Ashby said, and her expression suggested she suddenly was confronting a headful of questions.

"You weren't here when Timms finally did get home?" Dashee asked.

"I was back at my house. Then the next day, a car drove up with the two FBI men in it. They asked me if I'd heard an airplane flying over. I told them what I've told you. They wanted to know if anybody had come around the Timms place while I was there. I said no. That was about it."

That was about it for Dashee and Chee as well. They took a look at the barn, at the broken hasp, looked around for tracks and found nothing useful. Then they drove south through the dying red flare of twilight toward Mexican Water, where Eldon Timms had his other little place, where they dearly hoped, prayed, in fact, they would not find an L-17 hidden.

"If it's there," Dashee said, "then I tell the sheriff, and he tells the FBI, and old Eldon Timms gets sent up for insurance fraud and what else? Obstruction of justice?"

"Probably," Chee said. But he was thinking of three men, nameless, faceless, utterly unidentified, armed with automatic rifles. They had already killed a policeman, wounded another and tried to kill a third. Three killers at large in the Four Corners canyon country. He was wondering how many more would die before this thing was over.

NINE

THE LITTLE MAP Potts had drawn for Leaphorn on a sheet of notepaper took him across the San Juan down the asphalt of Highway 35 into the Aneth Oil Field, and thence onto a dirt road which led up the slopes of Casa Del Eco Mesa. It wandered past the roofless, windowless stone buildings which Potts had said were the relics of Jorie's ill-fated effort to run a trading post. Two dusty, bumpy miles later it brought him to the drainage that Potts had labeled Desert Creek. Leaphorn stopped there, let the dust settle a moment and looked down the slope. He saw a crooked line of pale green cottonwoods, gray-green Russian olives and silver-gray chamisa brush marking the course of the creek, the red roof of a house, a horse corral, sheep pens, a stack of hay bales protected by a vast sheet of plastic, and a windmill beside the round galvanized-metal form of the tank that received its water. Snaking down the slope along the road was a telephone line, sagging along between widely spaced poles.

Memory clicked in. He'd been there before. Now he knew why Jorie's name had rung a bell. He'd come to this ranch at least twenty-five years ago to deal with a complaint from a rancher that Jorie was shooting at him when he flew his airplane over. Jorie had been amiable about it. He had been shooting at crows, he said, but he sure did wish that Leaphorn would tell the fellow that flying so low over his place bothered his cattle. And apparently that had ended that—just another of the thousands of jobs rural policemen get solving little social problems among people turned eccentric by an overdose of dramatic skyscapes, endless silence and loneliness.

Leaphorn fished his binoculars from the glove box for a closer look. Nothing much had changed. The windmill tower now also supported what seemed to be an antenna, which meant Jorie—like many empty-country ranchers living beyond the reach of even Rural Electrification Administration power lines—had invested in radio communication. And the windmill was also rigged to turn a generator to provide the house with some battery-stored electricity. A little green tractor, dappled with rust and equipped with a front-end loader, was parked in the otherwise empty horse corral. No other vehicle was visible, which didn't mean one wasn't sitting somewhere out of sight.

Leaphorn found himself surprised by this. He'd expected to see a pickup, or whatever Jorie drove, parked by the house and Jorie working on something by one of the outbuildings. He'd expected to confirm that Jorie had not flown away with the Ute Casino loot and that Gershwin had been using him in some sort of convoluted scheme. He leaned back on the truck seat, stretched out his legs, and thought the whole business through again. A waste of time? Probably. How about dangerous? He didn't think so, but he'd have an explanation for this visit handy if Jorie came to the door and invited him in. He shifted the truck back into gear, drove slowly down the slope, parked under the cottonwood nearest the front porch and waited a few moments for his arrival to be acknowledged.

Nothing happened. No one appeared at the front door to note his arrival. He listened and heard nothing. He got out of the truck, closed the door carefully and silently, and walked toward the house, up the stone front steps, and tapped his knuckles against the doorframe. No response. A faint sound. Or had he imagined it?

"Hello," Leaphorn shouted. "Anyone home?"

No answer. He knocked again. Then stood, ear to the door, listening. He tried the knob, gently. Not locked, which wasn't surprising and didn't necessarily mean Jorie was home. Locking doors in this empty country was considered needless, fruitless and insulting to one's neighbors. If a thief wanted in, it would be about as easy to break the glass and climb in through a window.

But what was he hearing now?

A dim, almost imperceptible high note. Repeated. Repeated. Then a different sound. Something like a whistle. Birdsong? Now a bit of the music meadowlarks make at first flight. Leaphorn moved down the porch to a front window, shaded the glass with his hands and peered in. He looked into a dark room, cluttered with furniture, rows of shelved books, the dark shape of a television set.

He stepped off the end of the porch, walked around the corner of the house and stopped at the first window. The front of a green Ford 150 pickup jutted out from behind the house. Jorie's? Or someone else's? Perhaps Buddy Baker. Or Ironhand. Or both. Leaphorn became abruptly conscious that he was a civilian. That he didn't have the .38-caliber revolver he would have had with him if he was a law officer on duty. He shook his head. This uneasiness was groundless. He walked to the corner of the house. The truck was an oversize-cab model with no one visible in it. He reached through the open window and pulled down the sunshade. Clipped on it was the required liability insurance certification in Jorie's name. The cab was cluttered with trash, part of a newspaper, an Arby's sandwich sack, a bent drinking straw, three red poker chips—the twenty-five-dollar denomination bearing the Ute Casino symbol—on the passenger-side seat.

Leaphorn considered the implications of that a moment, then walked back to the house, put his forehead against the glass, shaded his eyes and looked into what seemed to be a bedroom also used as an office.

Once again he heard the birdcalls, more distinct now. To his right, close to the window, a single bright spot in the darkness attracted his eye. What seemed to be a small television screen presented the image of a meadow, a pond, a shady woods, birds. His eyes adjusted to the dimness. It was a computer monitor. He was seeing the screen saver. As he looked the scene shifted to broken clouds, a formation of geese. The birdsong became honking.

Leaphorn looked away from the screen to complete a scanning of the room. He sucked in his breath. Someone was slumped in the chair in front of the computer, leaning away, against an adjoining desk. Asleep? He doubted it. The position was too awkward for sleep.

Leaphorn hurried back across the porch, opened the door, shouted, "Hello. Hello. Anyone home?" and trotted through the living room into the bedroom.

The form in the chair was a small, gray-haired man, wearing a white T-shirt with HANG UP AND DRIVE printed across the back, new-looking jeans and bedroom slippers. His left arm rested on the tabletop adjoining the computer stand, and his head rested upon it with his face illuminated by the light from the monitor. The light brightened as the screen saver presented a new set of birds. That caused the color of the blood that had seeped down from the hole above his right eye to change from almost black to a dark red.

Everett Jorie, Leaphorn thought. *How long have you been dead? And how many years as a policeman does it take for me to get used to this? And understand it? And where is the person who killed you?*

He stepped back from Jorie's chair and surveyed the room, looking for the telephone and seeing it behind the computer with two stacks of the red Ute Casino chips beside it. Jorie was irrevocably dead. Calling the sheriff could wait for a few moments. First he would look around.

A pistol lay partly under the computer stand, beside the dead man's foot—a short-barreled revolver much like the one Leaphorn had carried before his retirement. If there was a smell of burned gunpowder in the room, it was too faint for him to separate from the mixed aromas of dust, the old wool rug under his feet, mildew and the outdoor scents of hay, horse manure, sage and dry-country summer invading through the open window.

Leaphorn squatted beside the computer, took his pen from his shirt pocket, knelt, inserted it into the gun barrel, lifted the weapon and inspected the cylinder. One of the cartridges it held had been fired. He took out his handkerchief, pushed the cylinder release and swung it open. The cartridge over the chamber was also empty. Perhaps Jorie had carried the pistol with the hammer over a discharged round instead of an empty chamber, a sensible safety precaution. Perhaps he didn't. That was something to be left to others to determine. He returned the pistol to its position beside the victim's foot, slid out the ballpoint, then stood for a moment, holding the pen and studying the room.

It held a small, neatly made double bed. Beyond the bed, an automatic rifle leaned against the wall, an AK-47. A little table beside it held a lamp, an empty water glass and two books. One was *The Virtue of Civility*, with the subtitle "Selected Essays on Liberalism." The other lay on its back, open.

Leaphorn checked the page, used the pen to

close it. The cover title read: *Cato's Letters: Essays on Liberty*. He flipped the book open again, remembering it from a political science course in his undergraduate days at Arizona State. Appropriate reading for someone trying to go to sleep. The bookshelves along the wall were lined with similar fare: J.F. Cooper's *The American Democrat*, Burke's *Further Reflections on the Revolution in France*, Sidney's *Discourses Concerning Government*, de Tocqueville's *Democracy in America*, along with an array of political biographies, autobiographies and histories. Leaphorn extracted *The Servile State* from its shelf, opened it and read a few lines for the sake of Hilaire Belloc's poetic polemics. He'd read that one and a few of the others thirty years or so ago in his period of fascination with political theory. Most of them were strange to him, but the titles were enough to tell him that he'd find no socialists among Jorie's heroes.

He located Jorie's telephone book in an out basket beside the phone, found he could still remember the proper sheriff's number and picked up the telephone receiver. From the computer came an odd gargling sound. The screen was displaying a long V of sandhill cranes migrating against a winter sky. Leaphorn put down the phone, took his ballpoint pen, and tapped the computer mouse twice.

The cranes and their gargling vanished—

instantly replaced on the screen by text. Leaphorn leaned past the body and read:

NOTICE: To anyone who might care, if such person exists, I declare I am about to close in appropriate fashion my wasted life. Fittingly, it ends with another betrayal. The sortie against the Ute Casino, which I foolishly believed would help finance our struggle against federal despotism, has served instead to finance only greed—and that at the needless cost of lives.

My only profit from this note will be revenge, which the philosophers have told us is sweet. Sweet or not, I trust it will remove from society two scoundrels, betrayers of trust, traitors to the cause of liberty and American ideals of freedom, civil rights and escape from the oppression of an arrogant and tyrannical federal government.

The traitors are George (Badger) Ironhand, a Ute Indian who runs cattle north of Montezuma Creek, and Alexander (Buddy) Baker, whose residence is just north of the highway between Bluff and Mexican Hat. It was Ironhand who shot the two victims at the casino and Baker who shot at the policeman near Aneth. Both of these shootings were in direct defiance of my orders and in violation of our plan, which was to obtain the cash collection from the casino without causing injury. We intended to take advantage of the confusion caused by the power failure and the darkness and to cause injury to no one. Both Ironhand and Baker were aware of the policy of gambling casinos, following the pattern set in Las Vegas, of instructing security guards not to use their weapons due to the risk of injury to clients and to the devastating publicity and loss of revenue such injuries would produce. Thus the deaths at the casino were unplanned, unprovoked, unnecessary and directly contrary to my instructions.

By the time we reached the point where we had planned to abandon the vehicle and return to our homes it had become clear to me that this violence had been privately planned by Ironhand and Baker and that their plan also included my own murder and their appropriation of the proceeds for their private and personal use. Therefore, I slipped away at the first opportunity.

I have no apologies for the operation. Its cause was just—to finance the continued efforts of those of us who value our political freedom more than life itself, to forward our campaign to save the American Republic from the growing abuses of our socialist government, and to foil its conspiracy to subject American citizens to the yoke of a world government.

It would not serve our cause for me to stand the pseudo-trial which would follow my arrest. The servile media would use it to make patriots appear to be no more than robbers. I prefer to sentence myself to death rather than endure either a public execution or life imprisonment.

However, arrest of Ironhand and Baker and the recovery of the casino proceeds they have taken would demonstrate to the world that their murderous actions were those of two common criminals seeking their own profits and not the intentions of patriots. If you do not find them at their homes, I suggest you check Recapture Creek Canyon below the Bluff Bench escarpment and just south of the White Mesa Ute Reservation. Ironhand has relatives and friends among the Utes there, and I have heard him talking to Baker about a free-flowing spring and an abandoned sheepherder's shack there.

I must also warn that after the business was done at the casino, these two men swore a solemn oath in my presence not to be taken alive. They accused me of cowardice and boasted that they would kill as many policemen as they could. They said that if they were ever surrounded and threatened with capture, they would continue killing police under the pretext of surrendering.

Long Live Liberty and all free men. Long live America.

I now die for it.

Everett Emerson Jorie

Leaphorn read through the text again. Then he picked up the telephone, dialed the sheriff's office number, identified himself, asked for the officer in charge and described what he had found at the residence of Everett Jorie.

"No use for an ambulance," Leaphorn said. And yes, he would wait until officers arrived and make sure that the crime scene was not disturbed.

That done, Leaphorn walked slowly through the rest of Jorie's home—looking but not touching. Back in Jorie's office, the sandhill cranes were again soaring across the computer screen saver, projecting an odd flickering illumination on the walls of the twilight room. Leaphorn tapped the mouse with his pen again, and reread the text of Jorie's note a third time. He checked the printer's paper supply, clicked on the PRINT icon, and folded the printout into his hip pocket. Then he went out onto the front porch and sat, watching the sunset give the thunderclouds on the western horizon silver fringes and turn them into yellow flame and dark red, and fade away into darkness.

Venus was bright in the western sky when he heard the police cars coming.

TEN

JIM CHEE TURNED down a side road on the high side of Shiprock and parked at a place offering a view of both the Navajo Tribal Police district office beside Highway 666 and his own trailer house under the cottonwoods beside the San Juan River. He got out, focused his binoculars and examined both locations.

As he feared, the NTP lot was crowded with vehicles, including New Mexico State Police black-and-whites, some Apache and Navajo County Sheriffs' cars, and three of those shiny black Fords instantly identifiable by all, cops and criminals alike, as the unmarked cars used by the FBI. It was exactly what the newscasts had led him to expect. The word was out that the missing L-17 had been found resting in a hay shed near Red Mesa. Thus the fervent hope of all Four Corners cops that the Ute Casino bandits had flown away to make themselves someone else's problem in another and far-distant jurisdiction had been dashed. That meant leaves would be canceled, everybody would be working overtime—including Sergeant Jim Chee unless he could keep out of sight and out of touch.

He focused on his own place. No vehicles were parked amid the cottonwoods that shaded his house trailer, so maybe no one was there waiting to order him back to duty. Chee had time left on his leave. He'd spent the morning making the long drive to the west slope of the Chuska range and then into high country to the place where Hosteen Frank Sam Nakai had always spent his summers tending his sheep, and where he now spent them doing the long slide into death by lung cancer. But Nakai wasn't there. And neither was his wife, Blue Woman, nor their truck.

Chee was disappointed. He'd wanted to tell Nakai that he'd been right about Janet Pete—that marriage with his beautiful, chic, brilliant silver-spoon socialite lawyer would never work. Either she would give up her ambitions, stay with him in *Dinetah* and be miserable, or he'd take the long bitter step out of the Land Between the Sacred Mountains and become a miserable success. In his gentle, oblique way, Nakai had tried to show him that, and he wanted to tell the man that he'd finally seen it for himself. Chee hung around for a while, thinking Nakai would be back soon. Even with his cancer in one of its periodic remissions, he wouldn't be strong enough for any extended travels. Certainly Nakai wouldn't be strong enough to conduct any of the curing ceremonial that his role as a *yataalii* required of him.

When the sun dipped behind the thunderheads over Black Mesa on the western horizon, Chee gave up and headed home. He would try again tomorrow unless Captain Largo located him. If that happened, he'd be spending what was left of his vacation trudging up and down canyons, serving as live bait for three fellows armed with automatic rifles and a demonstrated willingness to shoot cops.

Now he put his binoculars back into their case, drove down the hill and left his pickup behind a screen of junipers behind his trailer. A note was fastened to his screen door with a bent paper clip.

"Jim—The Captain says for you to report in right away."

Chee repinned it to the door and went in. The light on his telephone answering machine was blinking. He sat, took off his boots, and punched the answering-machine button.

The voice was Cowboy Dashee's:

"Hey, Jim. I filled the sheriff in on us finding

Old Man Timms's airplane. He called the feds, they got me on the phone, too. (Sound of Cowboy chuckling) The agent quizzing me didn't want to believe it was the same airplane, and I don't blame him. I didn't want to believe it either. Anyway, they sent somebody down there to make sure us indigenous people can tell an old L-17 from a zeppelin, and now the same old manhunt circus is getting organized just like in '98. If you want to save what's left of your vacation, I'd recommend you keep a long way from your office."

The next call was brief.

"This is Captain Largo. Get your ass down here. The feds located that damned airplane, and we're going to be the beagles on one of their fox hunts again." Largo, who normally sounded grouchy, sounded even grouchier than usual.

The third call was his insurance dealer telling him he needed to add an uninsured motorists clause to his policy. The fourth and final one was Officer Bernadette Manuelito.

"Jim. I talked to Cowboy, and he told me what you did. And I want to thank you for that. But I was at the hospital in Farmington this morning, and they have Hosteen Nakai there. He's very sick, and he told me he needs to see you. I'm going to come by your place. It's ah, it's almost six. I should be there by six-thirty or so."

Chee spent a moment considering what Bernie had said. Then he erased calls one, three and four, leaving the Largo call (in case the captain needed to think he hadn't heard it). Why would Nakai be in the hospital? It was hard to imagine that. He was dying of lung cancer, but he would never, never want to die in a hospital. Nakai was an ultra-traditional. A famous *yataalii*, a shaman who sang the Blessing Way, the Mountain Top Chant, the Night Way, and other curing ceremonials. As the older brother of Chee's mother, he was Chee's "little father," the one who had given Chee his secret "war name," his mentor, the tutor who had tried to teach Chee to be a singer himself. Hosteen Nakai would hate being in a hospital. Dying in such a place would be intolerable for him. How could this have happened? Blue Woman was smart and tough. How could she have allowed anyone to take her husband from their place in the Chuska Mountains?

He was trying to think of an answer to that when he heard the sound of tires on gravel, looked up and saw through the screen door Bernie's pickup rolling to a stop. Maybe she could tell him.

She couldn't.

"I just happened to see him," Bernie said. "They rolled him up on a gurney to where I was waiting for the elevator, and I thought he looked like your uncle, so I asked him if he was Hosteen Nakai, and he nodded, and I told him I worked with you, and he reached out for my arm and said to tell you to come, and I said I would, and then he said to tell you to come right away. And then the elevator came, and they put him on it." Bernie shook her head, her expression sad. "He looked bad."

"That was all he said? Just for me to hurry and come?"

She nodded again. "I went back to the nursing station and asked. The nurse said they had put him in Intensive Care. She said it was lung cancer."

"Yes," Chee said. "Did she say how he got there?"

"She said an ambulance had brought him in. I guess his wife checked him in." She paused, looked at Chee, down at her hands and at him again. "The nurse said it was terminal. He had a tube in his arm and an oxygen thing."

"It's been terminal a long time," Chee said. "Cancer. Another victim of the demon cigarette. Last time I saw him they thought he had just a few weeks to live and that was—" He stopped, thinking it had been months. Far too long. He felt shame for that—for violating the bedrock rule of the Navajo culture and putting his own interests ahead of family needs. Bernie was watching him, awaiting the end of his sentence. Looking slightly untidy as usual, and worried, and a little shy, wearing jeans stiff with newness and a bit too large for her and a shirt which fit the same description. A pretty girl, and nice, Chee thought, and found himself comparing her with Janet. Comparing pretty with beautiful, cute with classy, a sheep-camp woman with high society. He sighed. "That was far too long ago," he concluded, and looked at his watch.

"They have evening visiting hours," he said, and got up. "Maybe I can make it by then."

"I wanted to tell you I talked to Cowboy Dashee," Bernie said. "He told me what you did."

"Did? You mean the airplane?"

"Yes," she said, looking embarrassed. "That was a lot of work for you. You were sweet to do all that."

"Oh," Chee said. "Well. It was mostly luck."

"I guess that was the big reason they were holding Teddy. Because he could fly. And he knew the man who had the plane. I owe you a big favor now. I didn't really mean to ask you to do all that work. I just wanted you to tell me what to do."

"I was going to ask why you were at the hospital. Seeing about Teddy Bai, I guess."

"He's better now," she said. "They moved him out of Intensive Care."

"I didn't know Bai knew Eldon Timms," Chee said. "Did you know that?"

"Janet Pete told me," Bernie said. "She was at the hospital. She was appointed to represent Teddy."

"Oh," Chee said. Of course. Janet was a lawyer in the federal court public defender's office. Bai was a Navajo. So was Janet, by her father's name and her father's blood if not by conditioning. Naturally, they'd give her Bai's case.

Bernie was studying him. "She asked about you,"

"Oh?"

"I told her you were on vacation. Just back from going fishing up in Alaska."

"Uh, what did she say to that?"

"She just sort of laughed. And she said she'd heard you had a hand in finding that airplane. Said she guessed you must have been doing that on your own time. I hadn't talked to Cowboy yet, and I didn't know about that, so I just said, well anyway you hadn't gone back to work yet. And she laughed again, and said she thought getting egg on the FBI's face had become sort of a hobby with you."

Chee picked up his hat. "It's not," he said. "Lot of good people in the Bureau. It's just they let the FBI get way too big. And the politicians get the promotions, and so they're the ones making the policies and calling the shots instead of the bright ones. And so a lot of stupid things happen."

"Like evacuating Bluff in that big manhunt of '98," Bernie said.

Chee held the door open for her.

Bernie stood there looking at him, in no hurry to leave.

"Would you like to go along?" Chee asked. "Go see Hosteen Nakai with me?"

Bernie's expression said she would.

"Could I help?"

"Maybe. Be good company anyway. And you could bring me up to date on what I've been missing here."

But Bernie wasn't very good company. As soon as she climbed into his pickup and shut the door behind her, he said, "You mentioned Janet asked about me at the hospital. What else did she say?"

Bernie looked at him a moment. "About you?"

"Yeah," Chee said, wishing he hadn't asked that question.

She thought for a moment, either about what Janet Pete had said about him, or about what she was willing to tell him.

"Just what I told you already, about you liking to embarrass the FBI," she said.

After that there wasn't much talking during the thirty-mile drive to the hospital.

Visiting hours were almost over when they pulled into the parking lot, and the traffic was mostly outgoing.

"I was noticing faces," Bernie said. "The ones who had good news and the ones who didn't. Not many of them looked happy."

"Yeah," Chee said, thinking of how he could apologize to Hosteen Nakai for neglecting him, trying to come up with the right words.

"Hospitals are always so sad," Bernie said. "Except for the maternity ward."

It took only a glance at the nurse manning the desk on the floor housing the Intensive Care ward to support Bernie's observation. She was talking on a desk telephone, a graying, middle-aged woman whose face and voice reflected sorrow.

"Did he say when? OK." She glanced up at Chee and Bernie, gave the "just a moment" signal, and said, "When he checks in tell him the Morris boy died." She hung up, made a wry face and replaced it with a question.

"We've come to see Mr. Frank Sam Nakai," Chee said.

"He may not be awake," she said, and glanced at the clock. "Visiting hours end at eight. You'll have to make it brief."

"He sent a message," Chee said. "He asked me to come right away."

"Let's see then," she said, and led them down the hall.

It was hard to tell whether Nakai was awake,

or even alive. Much of his face was covered with a breathing mask, and he lay absolutely still.

"I think he's sleeping," Bernie said, and as she said it, Nakai's eyes opened. He turned his face toward them and removed the mask.

"Long Thinker has come," he said, in Navajo and in a voice almost too weak to be audible.

"Yes, Little Father," Chee said. "I am here. I should have come long ago."

A slender translucent tube connected Hosteen Nakai to a plastic container hung on a bedside stand. Nakai's fingers followed the tube along the sheet to his arm. Not the burly arm Chee remembered. Not much more than a bone covered with dry skin.

"I will go away soon," Nakai said. He spoke with his eyes closed, in slow, careful Navajo. "The instanding wind will be leaving me, and I will follow it to another place." He tapped his forearm with a finger. "Nothing will be left here but these old bones then. Before that, I must tell something. There is something I left unfinished. I must give you the last of your lessons."

"Lesson?" Chee asked, but instantly he knew what Nakai meant. Years ago, when Chee had still believed he could be both a Navajo Policeman and a *yataalii*, Nakai had been teaching him how to do the Night Way ceremony. Chee had memorized the actions of the Holy People involved in myth and how to reproduce this story in the sand paintings. He'd sung the chants that told the story. He'd learned the formula for the emetic required, how to handle the patient, everything required to produce the magic that would compel the Holy People to end the sickness and restore the harmony of natural life. Everything except the last lesson.

The tradition of Navajo shamanism required that. The teacher withheld the ultimate secret until he was certain the student was ready for it. For Chee, that moment had never come. Once he had gone away to Virginia to study at the FBI Academy, once he had flown to Los Angeles to work on a case, once he'd gone to Nakai's winter hogan to be tutored and Nakai had said the season and the weather were wrong for it. Finally, Chee had concluded that Nakai had seen that he would never be ready to sing the Night Way. He had been hurt by that. He had suspected that Nakai disapproved of assimilation of the white man's ways, of his plan to marry Janet Pete, had understood that having a Navajo father would never prepare her for the sacrifices required of a shaman's wife. Whatever the reason, Chee had respected Nakai's wisdom. He would have to forget that boyhood dream. He was not to be entrusted with the power to cure. He had come to accept that.

But now—? Had Nakai changed his mind? What could he say?

"Here?" he said. He gestured at the white, sterile walls. "Could you do that here?"

"A bad place," Nakai said. "Many people have died here, and many are sick and unhappy. I hear them crying in the hallway. And the *chindi* of the dead are trapped within its walls. I hear them, too. Even when they give me the medicine that makes me sleep, I hear them. What I must teach you should be done in a holy place, far away from evil. But we have no choice."

He replaced the mask over his face, inhaled oxygen, and removed it again.

"The *bilagaana* do not understand death," he said. "It is the other end of the circle, not something that should be fought and struggled against. Have you noticed that people die just at the end of night, when the stars are still shining in the west and you can sense the brightness of Dawn Boy on the eastern mountains? That's so the Holy Wind within them can go to bless the new day. I always thought I would die like that. In the summer. At our camp in the Chuskas. With the stars above me. With my instanding wind blowing free. Not dying trapped in—"

Nakai's voice had become so faint that Chee couldn't understand the last words. Then it faded into silence.

Chee felt Bernie's touch at his elbow.

"Jim. If this is something ceremonial, shouldn't I leave?"

"I guess so," Chee said. "I really don't know."

They stood, watching Nakai, his eyes closed now.

Chee replaced the oxygen mask over his face, felt Bernie's touch on his elbow.

"He hates this place," Bernie said. "Let's get him out of here."

"What do you mean?" Chee said. "How?"

"We tell the nurse we're taking him home. And then we take him home."

"What about all that?" Chee asked, pointing at the oxygen mask, the tubes that tied Nakai to life, and the wires that linked him to the computers which measured the Holy Wind within him and reduced it to electronic blips racing across television screens. "He'll die."

"Of course he'll die," Bernie said, her tone impatient. "That's what the nurse told us. He's dying right now. That's what he was telling you. But he doesn't want to die here."

"You're right," Chee said. "But how do—"

But Bernie was walking out. "First, I call the ambulance service," she said. "While they're coming I'll start trying to check him out."

It was not quite as simple as Bernie made it

sound. The nurse was sympathetic but had questions to be answered. For example, where was Nakai's wife, whose name, but not her signature, was on the admissions form? By what authority were they taking Mr. Nakai off the life-support systems and out of the hospital? The doctor who had admitted Mr. Nakai had left for Albuquerque. That shifted responsibility to another doctor—now busy in the emergency room downstairs patching up a knifing victim. He arrived on the floor thirty minutes and two paging calls later, looking young and tired.

"What's this about?" he asked, and the nurse provided a fill-in that caused him to look doubtful. Meanwhile, the ambulance attendant emerged from the elevator, recognized Chee from working traffic accidents and asked him for instructions.

"I can't do it," the doctor said. "The patient's on life support. We need authorization from the next of kin. Lacking that, the admitting physician needs to sign him out."

"That's not really the question," Chee said. "We are taking Hosteen Nakai home tonight to be with his wife. Our question is how you can help us do this to minimize the trouble it might cause."

That produced a chilly but brief silence followed by the signing by Chee of a Released Against

Advice of Physician form and a financial responsibility statement. Then Hosteen Frank Sam Nakai was free again.

Chee rode in the back of the ambulance with Nakai and the emergency medical technician.

"I guess you heard they got one of those casino bandits," the tech said. "It was on the six o'clock news."

"No," Chee said. "What happened?"

"The guy shot himself," the tech said. "It was that fella that used to have a radio talk show. Sort of a right-winger. News said he ran cattle up there south of Aneth. Married a Navajo woman and was using her grazing allotment up there."

"Shot himself? What'd they say about that?"

"Not much. It was at his house. I guess they were closing in on him, and he didn't want to get arrested. Fella named Everett Jorie. And now they know who the other two were. Said they're both from up there in Utah. Part of one of those militia bunches."

"Jorie," Chee said. "Never heard of him."

"He used to have a talk show on the radio. You know, all the nuts calling in and complaining about the government."

"OK. I remember him now."

"And they have the other two identified now. Man named George Ironhand and one named

Buddy Baker. I think Ironhand's a Ute. Anyway, they said he used to work at the Ute Casino."

"I wonder how they got them identified."

"The TV said the FBI did it, but it didn't say how."

"Well, hell," Chee said. "I was hoping they'd catch them in Los Angeles, or Tulsa, or Miami, or anyplace a long ways from this place."

The ambulance tech chuckled. "You're not anxious to go prowling around in those canyons again. I wouldn't be, either."

Chee let that pass into silence.

Then Hosteen Nakai sighed, and said, "Ironhand." And sighed again.

Chee leaned over him, and said, "Little Father. Are you all right?"

"Ironhand," Nakai said. "Be careful of him. He was a witch."

"A witch? What did he do?"

But Hosteen Nakai seemed to be sleeping again.

ELEVEN

THE HALF MOON was dipping behind the mountains to the west when the ambulance, with Bernie trailing it in Chee's truck, rolled down the track and stopped outside Hosteen Nakai's sheep-camp place in the Chuskas. Blue Woman was standing in the doorway waiting. She ran out to greet them, crying. At first the tears were for grief, thinking they were bringing home her husband's body. Then she cried for joy.

They put him on his bed beside a piñon tree, rearranged his oxygen supply and listened to Blue Woman's tearful explanation of how Hosteen Nakai had come to be abandoned, as she saw it, in the Farmington hospital. Her niece had come to take her to have an infected tooth removed, and to replenish the supply of the medicine which kept away the pain and let her husband sleep. Nakai had been much better, had wanted to come along and there had been no one to look after him at the sheep camp. But at the dentist's office he had fainted, someone called 911, and an ambulance took him to the hospital. She had waited there, and waited, not knowing what to do for him, and finally her niece had to go to care for her children, and she had to go with her. There were stories that the rich young people from the cities were putting wolves back in the mountains, and there was no one at their place to protect their young lambs.

Nakai was awake now, listening to all this. When Blue Woman was finished, he motioned to Chee.

"I have something to tell you," he said. "A story."

"We will make some coffee," Blue Woman said. She led Bernie away to the hogan, and as they left Nakai began his tale.

It would be long, Chee thought, involving the intricacies of Navajo theology, the relationship of the universal creator who set all nature in its harmonious motion to the spirit world of the Holy People, and to humanity, and when it was finished he would know the final secret that would qualify him as a shaman.

"I think you will be going into the canyon soon

to hunt the men who killed the policemen," Nakai said. "I must tell you a story about Ironhand. I think you must be very, very careful."

Chee exhaled a long breath. *Wrong again*, he thought.

"A long time ago when I was a boy, and the winter stories were being told in the hogan, and people were talking about the great dam that was going to make Lake Powell, and how the water of the Colorado and the San Juan were backing up and drowning the canyons, the old men would talk about how the Utes and the Paiutes would come through the canyons in their secret ways, and steal the sheep and horses of our people, and kill them, too. And the worst of these was a Paiute they called Dobby, and the band that followed him. And the worst of the Utes was a man they called Ironhand."

Nakai replaced his oxygen mask and spent a few moments inhaling.

"Ironhand," Chee said, probably too softly for Nakai to hear him.

Nakai removed the mask again.

"They say Dobby and his people came out of the canyons at night and stole the sheep and horses at the place of woman of the *tl'igu dinee*, and they killed her and her daughter and two children. And the son-in-law of this old woman was a man they called Littleman, who married into the Salt

Clan but was born to the Near the Water *Dine'*. And they say he forgot the Navajo Way and went crazy with his grief."

Nakai's voice grew weaker, and slower, as he related how Littleman, after years spent hunting and watching, had finally found the narrow trail the raiders had used and finally killed Dobby and his men.

"It took summer after summer for many years for the Salt Clan to catch Dobby," Nakai said. "But no one ever caught the Ute they called Ironhand."

The moon was down, the dark sky overhead adazzle with stars, and Chee was feeling the high-altitude chill. He leaned forward in his chair and tucked the blankets around Nakai's shoulders.

"Little Father," he said, "I think you should sleep now. Do you need more of the medicine for that?"

"I need you to listen," Nakai said. "Because while our people never caught Ironhand, we know now why we didn't. And we know he had a son and a daughter, and I think he must have a son or a grandson. And I think that is who you will be hunting, and what I will tell you will help."

Chee had to lean forward now, his ear close to Nakai's lips, to hear the rest of it. After two of his raids, the Navajos had managed to trace Ironhand and his men into the Gothic Creek Canyon, and then down Gothic toward the San Juan under the rim of Casa Del Eco Mesa. There tracks turned into a steep, narrow side canyon where the Utes and Mormon settlers from Bluff dug coal. They found a corpse in one of the coal mines. But the canyon was a dead end with no way out. It was as if Ironhand and his men were witches who could fly over the cliffs.

Nakai's voice died away. He replaced the mask, inhaled, and removed it again.

"I think if there is a young man named Ironhand, he robs and kills people, he would know where his grandfather hid in that canyon, and how he escaped from it.

"And now," Hosteen Nakai said, "before I sleep, I must teach you the last lesson so you can be a *yataalii*." He took a labored breath. "Or not be one."

To Chee, the old man seemed utterly exhausted. "First, Father, I think you should rest and restore yourself. You should—"

"I must do it now," Nakai said. "And you must listen. The last lesson is the one that matters. Will you hear me?"

Chee took the old man's hand.

"Know that it is hard for the people to trust outside their own family. Even harder when they are sick. They have pain. They are out of harmony. They see no beauty anywhere. All their connections are broken. That is who you are talking to. You tell them the Power that made us made all this above us and around us and we are part of the Power and if we do as we are taught we can bring ourselves back into *hozho*. Back into harmony. Then they will again know beauty all around them."

Nakai closed his eyes, gripped Chee's hand.

"That is hard to believe," he said. "Do you understand that?"

"Yes."

"To be restored, they must believe you."

Nakai opened his eyes, stared at Chee.

"Yes," Chee said.

"You know the chants. You sing them without a mistake. And your sand paintings are exactly right. You know the herbs, how to make the emetics, all that."

"I hope so," Chee said, understanding now what Hosteen Frank Sam Nakai was telling him.

"But you have to decide if you have gone too far beyond the four Sacred Mountains. Sometimes you can never come all the way back into *Dinetah* again."

Chee nodded. He remembered a Saturday night after he'd graduated from high school. Nakai had driven him to Gallup. They had parked on Railroad Avenue and sat for two hours watching the drunks wandering in and out of the bars.

He'd asked Nakai why he'd parked there, who they were looking for. Nakai hadn't answered at first, but what he said when he finally spoke Chee had never forgotten.

"We are looking for the *dine'* who have left *Dinetah*. Their bodies are here, but their spirits are far beyond the Sacred Mountains. You can go east of Mount Taylor to find them, or west of the San Francisco Peaks, or you can find them here."

Chee had pointed to a man who had been leaning clumsily against the wall up the avenue from them, and who now was sitting, head down on the sidewalk. "Like him?" he asked.

Nakai had waved his hand in a motion that included the bar's neon Coors sign and the drunk now trying to push himself up from the pavement. But went beyond them to follow a polished white Lincoln Town Car rolling up the avenue toward them.

"Which one acts like he has no relatives?" Nakai had asked him. "The drunk who leaves his children hungry, or the man who buys that car that boasts of his riches instead of helping his brother?"

Nakai's eyes were closed now, and his efforts to breathe produced a faint groaning sound. Then he said, "To cure them you must make them believe. You must believe so strongly that they feel it. Do you understand?"

"Yes," Chee said. Nakai was telling him he had

failed to meet Nakai's standards as a shaman whose conduct of the curing ways would actually cure. And Nakai was forgiving him—freeing him to be the sort of modern man he was becoming. There was a sense of relief in that, mixed with a dreary sense of loss.

TWELVE

It was just a bit after noon when Captain Largo caught him.

Through his dreams Chee heard the sound of something thumping, which gradually became pounding, which suddenly was augmented by an angry shout.

"Damn it, Chee, I know you're in there. Unlock the door."

Chee unlocked the door and stood, naked except for boxer shorts and befuddled by sleep, staring at the captain.

"Where the hell have you been?" Largo demanded, pushing past Chee into the trailer. "And why don't you answer your telephone?"

The captain was staring at the telephone as he said it, noticing the little red light blinking on the answering machine.

"I've been away," Chee said. "Just got back, and I had a lot of family business to take care of."

He reached over, punched the button, awake enough now to be glad he'd been smart enough to erase the call from Cowboy Dashee. The machine reproduced the grouchy voice of Captain Largo saying: "This is Captain Largo. Get your ass down here. The feds located that damned airplane, and we're going to be the beagles on one of their fox hunts again."

The machine showed two other calls waiting and Chee clicked it off before they, whatever they were, got him into any trouble.

"I should have listened to that," he said. "But I just got in about nine this morning, and I was worn out." He told Largo how he and Officer Manuelito had brought his mother's oldest brother home from the hospital, about how the old man had managed to hold death at bay until he saw sunlight on the mountaintop, how Bernadette had gone to bring Blue Woman's sisters to help prepare the body for the traditional funeral. Under his uniform Largo was a traditional, a Standing Rock *Dine'*. He recalled the old man's fame as a singer and his wisdom and, like Chee himself, avoided speaking the name of the dead. He offered Chee his condolences, sat on the edge of Chee's fold-down cot, shook his head.

"I'd give you some time off if I could," he said,

ignoring the fact that Chee was officially still on vacation, "but you know how it is. We've got everybody out looking for those bastards, so I'm just going to give you a minute to get your uniform on, and while you do that I'll fill you in, and then I want you out there getting things a little better organized."

"OK," Chee said.

A sudden and unpleasant thought struck the captain. "Manuelito was with you, then," Largo said, looking murderous. "She didn't bother to tell me, though. Did she bother to tell you I was looking all over for you?"

"I didn't ask her," Chee said, and busied himself getting his pants on, buttoning his shirt, hoping Largo wouldn't notice how he'd evaded the question, thinking of nothing to say to take the heat off Bernie, and now, happy to see the captain heading out the door.

"I'll bring you up to speed in my office," Largo said. "In exactly thirty minutes."

Approximately thirty minutes later Chee was sitting in the chair in front of Largo's desk, listening to the captain's end of a telephone conversation. "OK," the captain said. "Sure. I understand. Will do. OK." He hung up, sighed, looked at Chee and his watch. "All right," he said. "Here's the situation."

Largo was good at it. He named and described

the surviving suspects. Nobody was at home at either man's residence. None of the neighbors had seen either man since before the robbery, which meant absolutely nothing in Ironhand's case because the nearest neighbor lived about four miles away. A horse trailer and two horses seemed to be missing from Ironhand's place. Since nobody could guess when or why, that might be equally meaningless. With their airplane-escape theory shot down, the feds had resumed custody of the manhunt operation, roadblocks were up and trackers were working over the area around the spot where the suspects had abandoned the escape vehicle.

"Pretty much Ringling Brothers, Barnum and Bailey again," Largo said. "Three sets of state police involved, three sheriff's departments, probably four, BIA cops, Ute cops, cops over from the Jicarilla Reservation, Immigration and Naturalization is sending up its Border Patrol trackers, federals galore, even Park Service security people. I'm putting you in Montezuma Creek. We have four people up there working with the FBI trying to locate some tracks. You're reporting to Special Agent"—Largo consulted a notepad on his desk—"named Damon Cabot. I don't know him."

"I've heard of him," Chee said. "You remember that old poem: 'The Lodges spoke only to Cabots, and the Cabots spoke only to God.' "

"No, I don't," Largo said, "and I hope you're not going up there with that smart-aleck attitude."

Chee looked at his watch. "You want me up there today?"

"I wanted you up there yesterday," Largo said. "Be careful and keep in touch."

"OK," Chee said, and headed for the door.

"And Chee," Largo said. "Use your head for once. Don't get crosswise with the Bureau again. Have some manners. Give 'em some respect."

Chee nodded.

Largo was grinning at him. "If you have trouble giving 'em respect, just remember they get paid about three times more than you do."

"Yeah," Chee said. "That'll help."

The gathering place for the manhunt was the conference room of the Montezuma Creek Chapter House. The parking lot was crowded with a varied assortment of police cars, most easily identified by jurisdiction by Chee. He spotted Cowboy Dashee's Apache County patrol unit resting off the gravel but under the shade of the lot's solitary tree, a couple NTP units, two of the shiny black Ford sedans the FBI used and an equally shiny green Land Rover. That, he concluded, would be far too expensive to be owned by any of the non-federal agencies here. Probably it had been seized in a drug raid and driven down from Salt Lake or

Denver by whichever Special Agent had been put in charge of this affair.

The conference room itself was as crowded as the lot and almost as hot. Someone had concluded that the feeble window-mounted air-conditioning unit wasn't handling the body heat produced by the crowd and had opened windows. A dozen or so men, some in camouflage outfits, some in uniforms, some in suits, were crowded around a table. Chee saw Dashee perched on a folding chair beside one of them, reading something.

Chee walked over. "Hey there, fella," he said to Dashee. "Are you the Special Agent in Charge?"

"Keep your voice down," Cowboy said. "I don't want the feds to know I associate with you. Not until this business is over, anyway. However, the man you want to report to is that tall guy with the black baseball cap with FBI on it. That doesn't stand for Full Blood Indian."

"He looks sort of young. Do you think he understands this country?"

Dashee laughed. "Well, he asked me about the trout fishing in the San Juan. He said somebody told him it was great. I think he's based in St. Louis."

"You tell him fishing was good?"

"Come on, Chee. Ease up. I just told him it was great about two hundred miles upstream before all the muddy irrigation water gets dumped in. He seems like a good guy. Said he was new out here. Didn't know whether to call a gully an ar-royo, or a wash, or a cut, or a creek. His name's Damon Cabot."

Up close Damon Cabot looked even younger than he had from the back of the room. He shook hands with Chee, explained that other detachments were handling other aspects of the hunt and that this group was trying to collect all possible evidence from the area where the escape vehicle had been abandoned.

"Here's where we have you," he said, pointing to the map spread on the table and indicating a red X near the center of Casa Del Eco Mesa. "That's our Truck Base. Where the perps abandoned the pickup truck. Are you familiar with that area?"

"Just generally," Chee said. "I worked mostly out of Shiprock and in the Tuba City district. That's way west of here."

"Well, you know it a hell of a lot better than I do," Cabot said. "I just got reassigned from Philadelphia to Salt Lake City about a week ago. Did you work in that 1998 manhunt?"

Chee nodded.

"From what I've been overhearing, the Bureau didn't add any luster to its reputation with that one."

Chee shrugged. "Nobody did."

"What do you think? Are those two guys still out there?"

"From 1998? Who knows? But a lot of people around here think so," Chee said.

"I guess the Bureau decided they're dead," Cabot said. "I just wondered—" He cut that off, and shifted into telling Chee how the fugitives were thought to be armed: assault rifles and perhaps at least one scoped hunting rifle. Chee noticed that Special Agent Cabot seemed slightly downcast. The man had been trying to be friendly. The realization surprised Chee. It made him a bit ashamed of himself.

He brought that up with Cowboy as they drove in the deputy's patrol car to the meeting place on Casa Del Eco Mesa.

"Exactly what I've been telling you," Cowboy said. "You pick on the feds all the time. Hostile. I think it grows out of your basic and well-justified inferiority complex. There's a little envy mixed in there, too, I think. Healthy, good-looking guys, blow-dry haircuts, big salaries, good retirement, shiny shoes, Hollywood always making movies about them, heel-e-o-copters to fly around in, flak jackets, expense accounts, retirement pensions and"—Cowboy paused, gave Chee a sidewise glance—"and getting to associate with those real pretty Justice Department public-defender lawyers all the time."

Which was Cowboy's effort to open the subject of Janet Pete. Chee had once asked Cowboy to be his best man if Janet insisted on the white people's style of wedding Janet's mother wanted instead of the Navajo wedding Chee preferred. He never really explained to Cowboy how that affair had crashed and burned, and he wasn't going to do it now.

"How about you, Cowboy?" Chee said. "Nobody ever accused you of loving the federals. You're the one who told me the most popular course in the FBI Academy is Insufferable Arrogance 101."

"It's Arrogance 201 that's popular. They expect recruits to test out of 101. Anyhow, most of them are nice guys. Just a lot richer than us."

One of them was awaiting them at Truck Base, sitting in a black van, monitoring radio traffic with a book open on the seat beside him. He said the Special Agent running this part of the show had gone down in the canyon, and they were supposed to wait for instructions.

The radio tech pointed to the yellow police-line tape he'd parked beside.

"Don't go inside that," he said. "That's where the perps abandoned their truck. We can't have people messing that up until the crime-lab team signs off on it."

"OK," Cowboy said. "We'll just wait."

They leaned against Cowboy's patrol car.

"Why didn't you tell him you were the one who put up the tape?" Chee asked.

"Just being nice," Cowboy said. "You ought to try that. The feds respond well to kindness."

Chee let that one pass into a long silence, which he broke with a question.

"Have you heard how the Bureau got the perps identified? I know they announced it to the press, which means they're sure of 'em. So first I thought they'd found the inside man and got him to talk. This Teddy Bai guy they were holding at the hospital. Do you know if they got him to talk?"

"All I know is fourth-hand," Cowboy said. "I heard your old boss did it. Got the names for them."

"Old boss?"

"Joe Leaphorn," Dashee said. "The Legendary Lieutenant Leaphorn. Who else?"

"Be damned," Chee said. "How the devil could that have happened?" But he noticed that he wasn't really surprised.

"They said the sheriff got a call from some old friend from Aneth, or someplace like that—a former county cop named Potts. This Potts said Leaphorn came to his house and asked him about three men and then how to find this Jorie guy's place. Hour or so later Leaphorn calls the cops from Jorie's house and tells them Jorie's killed himself. That's all I know."

"Be damned," Chee said again. "How in hell does—"

"How long did you work for him?" Cowboy asked. "Three, four years?"

"Seemed longer," Chee said.

"So you know he's smart," Cowboy said. "Logical, thinks things out."

"Yeah," Chee said, sounding grumpy. "Everything fits into a pattern for him. Every effect has its cause. I told you about his map, didn't I? Full of different colored pins marking different sorts of things. He'd stick 'em in there marking off travel times, confluences, so forth. Looking for a pattern."

Chee paused, struck by a sudden thought. "Or lack of one," he added.

Cowboy looked at him. "Like what do you mean?"

"Like I just thought of something that doesn't fit here. Remember, you told me this truck abandoned here was an oversize cab job, right? And you found two sets of footprints around it. And three was the number of guys seen in the robbery."

"Right," Cowboy said. "So where's that leading?"

"So how did this Jorie get from here to his home up in Utah?"

Silence while Cowboy considered that. He sighed. "I don't know. How about they dropped him off at his house before they got here. Or how about he actually got out of the truck here, but he was very careful where he stepped."

"You think that's possible?"

"No. Not really. I'm pretty good at finding tracks."

The door of the communications van opened, and the tech leaned out.

"Cabot called in," he shouted. "Says you guys can take off now. He wants you back here in the morning. About daylight."

Dashee waved good-bye. The communications tech returned to his reading. Chee said, "Does this somehow remind you of our Great Manhunt of 1998?"

Dashee backed his car up to the track, turned it in the direction of the wandering road that would take them back to pavement.

"Hold it a minute," Chee said. "Let's sit here a little while where we can see the lay of the land and think about this."

"Think?" Dashee said. "You're not an acting lieutenant anymore. That thinking can get you in trouble." But he pulled the car off the track and turned off the ignition.

They sat. After a while Dashee said, "What are you thinking about? I'm thinking about how early we have to hit the floor tomorrow to get up by daylight. How about you?"

"I'm thinking this started out looking like a well-planned operation. Everything was timed out precisely." Chee looked at Dashee, meshed his fingers together. "Perfect precision," he said. "You agree."

Dashee nodded.

"The guy on the roof cuts the right wires at the right time. They use a stolen truck with the plates switched, shooting both of the competent security people. They leave total confusion behind, fixing it so they were far away from the scene before roadblocks were up, and so forth. Everything planned. Right?"

"And now this." Chee waved at the landscape in front of them, dunes stabilized by growths of Mormon tea, stunted junipers, needle grass, and then westward where the Casa Del Eco highlands dropped sharply away into a waste of eroded canyons.

"So?" Dashee asked.

"So why did they come here?"

"Tell me," Dashee said, "and then let's go back to Montezuma Creek and get a loaf of bread and some lunch meat at the store there and have our dinner."

"Well, first you think maybe they panicked. Figured they'd run into roadblocks if they stayed on the pavement, turned off here, found this old track dead-ended, and just took off."

"OK," Dashee said. "Let's go get something to eat."

"But that doesn't work because all three of them lived around here, and that Ironhand guy is a Ute. He'd know every road out here. They had a reason to come here."

"All right," Dashee said. "So they came here to steal Old Man Timms's airplane and fly out of our jurisdiction. The FBI liked that one. I liked that one. Everybody liked that one until you went and screwed it up."

"Call that reason number two, then, and mark it wrong. Now reason number three, currently in favor, is this is the place they had picked to climb down into the canyons and disappear."

Dashee restarted the engine. "Funny place for that, I'd say, but let's think about it while we eat."

"I'd guess this drainage wash here would take you down into Gothic Creek, and then you could follow it all the way down to the San Juan River Canyon, and then if you can get across the river you could go up Butler Wash to just about anywhere. Or downstream a few miles and turn south again up the Chinle Canyon. Lots of places to hide out, but this is sort of an awkward, out-of-the-way place to start walking."

Dashee shifted into second as they rolled down a rocky slope where the track connected to what the map called "unimproved road."

"If they planned to hole up in the canyons, I'll bet you they knew what they were doing," Dashee said.

"I guess so. But then how about Jorie getting out of the truck here and going right home. That's a long way to walk."

"Drop it," Dashee said. "After I eat something and my stomach stops growling at me, I'll explain it all to you."

"I want to know how Lieutenant Leaphorn got those identities," Chee said. "I'm going to find out."

THIRTEEN

CHEE SCANNED THE tables in the Anasazi Inn dining room twice. He had looked right past the corner table and the stocky old duffer sitting there with a plump middle-aged woman without recognizing Joe Leaphorn. When he did recognize him on the second take, it came as a sort of a shock. He had seen the Legendary Lieutenant in civilian attire before, but the image he carried in his mind was of Leaphorn in uniform, Leaphorn strictly businesslike, Leaphorn deep in thought. This fellow was laughing at something the woman with him had said.

Chee hadn't expected the woman—although he should have. When he'd called Leaphorn's home the answering machine had said, "I'll be in the Anasazi Inn dining room at eight." No preamble, no good-bye, just the ten words required.

TONY HILLERMAN

The Legendary Lieutenant at his efficient best, expecting a call, unable to wait for it, rewording his answering machine answer to deal with the problem, handling an affair of the heart, if such it was, just as he'd handle a meeting with a district attorney. The woman dining with him he now recognized as the professor from Northern Arizona University with whom Leaphorn seemed to have something or other going. He wasn't accustomed to thinking of Leaphorn in any sort of romantic situation. Or to seeing him laughing. That was rare.

What wasn't rare was the effect this man had on him. Chee had considered it on the drive down to Farmington, had decided he was probably over it by now. He'd had the same feeling as a boy when Hosteen Nakai began teaching him about the Navajo relationship with the world, and at the University of New Mexico when in the presence of the famed Alaska Jack Campbell, who was teaching him early Athabascan culture in Anthropology 209.

He'd tried to describe it to Cowboy, and Cowboy had said, "You mean like a rookie reporting for basketball practice with Michael Jordan, or like a seminary student put on a committee with the pope." And, yes, that was close enough. And no, he hadn't quite gotten over it.

Leaphorn spotted him, got up, waved him over,

said, "You remember Louisa, I'm sure," and asked him if he'd like something to drink. Chee, already wired with about six cups of coffee since breakfast, said he'd settle for iced tea.

"I figured out how you knew where to find me," Leaphorn said. "You called my house, and got my machine, and it played you the message I'd subbed in to tell Louisa where I'd meet her."

"Right," Chee said. "And that saved me about a hundred miles of driving. Getting all the way down to Window Rock. Two hundred, because I've got to get back to Montezuma Creek in the morning."

"We'll be going in that direction, too," Leaphorn said. "Professor Bourebonette's been using me as translator. She's interviewing an old woman over at the Beclabito Day School tomorrow."

They talked about that until the time came to order dinner.

"Did the desk give you the message I left for you?" Chee said.

"You want to know what I can tell you about the Ute Casino business," Leaphorn said. "Are you forgetting that I'm a civilian these days?"

"No," Chee said, and smiled. "Nor am I forgetting how you used to make your good-old-boy network deliver. And I hear it was you who provided the identification of those guys to the FBI."

"Where'd you hear that?"

"Got it from an Apache County deputy sheriff."

Leaphorn's expression suggested he knew which deputy.

"Anyway, it's like most rumors," Leaphorn said, and shrugged.

"You gentlemen want me to go powder my nose?" the professor asked. "Give you some privacy?"

"Not me," Leaphorn said, and Chee shook his head.

"What you mean is that it's partly true? According to the story I heard you went out to this Jorie fellow's place, found him dead, called in to report he'd committed suicide and gave the feds the names of his accomplices. Could you tell me how much of that is true?"

"You're working on this, I guess," Leaphorn said. "How much have they told you?"

"Not much," Chee said, and filled him in.

"They didn't tell you about the suicide note?"

"No," Chee said. "They didn't."

Leaphorn shook his head and looked disappointed. "Lot of good people work in the FBI," he said. "Lot of dumb ones, too, and the way it works as a bureaucracy gets bigger and bigger and bigger, the dumber you are the higher you rise. They get caught up in the Washington competition, where knowledge is power. That gets them obsessed with secrecy."

"I guess so," Chee said.

"This obsession for secrecy," Leaphorn said, shaking his head. "I used to work with a Special Agent named Kennedy," he added, no longer grinning. "A great cop, Kennedy. He explained to me how it grew out of the turf wars in Washington. The Bureau, and the Treasury cops, and CIA, and the Secret Service, and U.S. Marshal's Office, and the BIA, and Immigration and Naturalization cops, and about fifteen other federal law-enforcement agencies pushing and shoving each other for more money and more jurisdiction. 'Knowledge is Power,' Kennedy'd say, so you get conditioned not to tell anybody anything. They might steal the headlines, and the TV time, from your agency."

Chee nodded. "This suicide note," he said. "Anything in it I should know?" Leaphorn, he was thinking, must be showing his age, or too much living alone. He didn't used to ramble off into such digressions.

"Maybe. Maybe not. But how do you know if you don't know what's in it?"

"Well, I do have a question about this Jorie. I'd like to understand how he got home from where he and his buddies left their truck. And I'd like to know, if he was going home anyway, why he didn't just have them drop him off there?"

Leaphorn looked thoughtful.

"Just two men in the truck when it was abandoned, then? You found the tracks?"

"Not me," Chee said. "I wasn't back from vacation. Sheriff's department people. Cowboy Dashee, in fact. You remember him?"

"Sure," Leaphorn said. "And Cowboy said two sets of tracks around the truck?"

"He said two was all he found. He photographed them. One set of slick-soled boots with cowboy heels, one set that looked like those nonskid walking shoes."

Leaphorn thought about that. "What else did Dashee find?"

"Around the truck?"

"Or in it. Anything interesting."

"It was a stolen oil-field truck," Chee said. "Had all that sort of stuff in it. Wrenches, oily rags, so forth."

Leaphorn waited for more, made a wry, apologetic face.

"Remember how I used to be?" he said. "Always after you to give me all the details. Not leave anything out. Even if it didn't seem to mean anything."

Chee grinned. "I do," he said. "And I remember I used to resent it. Felt like it meant I couldn't do the thinking on my own. Come to think of it, I still do."

"It wasn't that," Leaphorn said, his face a little flushed. "It was just that a lot of times I'd have access to information you didn't have."

"Well, anyway, I didn't mention a girlie magazine in a door pocket, and some receipts for gasoline purchases, a broken radio in the truck bed, an oil-wipe rag and an empty Dr Pepper can."

Leaphorn thought, said, "Tell me about the radio."

"The radio? Dashee said it wouldn't play. It looked new. Looked expensive. But it didn't work. He figured the battery must be dead."

Leaphorn thought again. "Seems funny they'd go off and leave something like that. They must have brought it along for a reason. Probably wanted to use it to keep track of what the cops were doing. Did it have a scanner, so they could monitor police radio traffic?"

"Damn," Chee said. "Dashee didn't say, and I didn't think to ask him."

Leaphorn glanced at Professor Bourebonette, looking apologetic.

"Go ahead," she said. "I always wondered how you guys do your work."

"Not in a restaurant usually," Leaphorn said. "But I wish I had a map."

"Lieutenant," Chee said, reaching for his jacket

pocket, "can you imagine me coming in here to talk to you and not bringing a map?"

The waitress arrived while Leaphorn was spreading the map over the tablecloth. She made a patient face, took their orders and went away.

"OK," Leaphorn said. He drew a small, precise X. "Here we have Jorie's place. Now, where did the men get out of the pickup?"

"I'd say right here," Chee said, and indicated the spot with a tine of his fork.

"Right beside that unimproved road?"

"No. Several hundred yards down a slope. Toward that Gothic Creek drainage."

The map they were using was THE MAP, produced years ago by the Automobile Club of Southern California, adopted by the American Automobile Association as its "Guide to Indian Country" and meticulously revised and modified year by year as bankruptcy forced yet another trading post to close, dirt roads became paved, flash floods converted "unimproved" routes to "impassable," and so forth. Leaphorn refolded it now to the mileage scale, transferred that to the margin of his paper napkin and applied that to measure the spaces between X's.

"About twenty miles as the crow flies," Leaphorn said. "Make it thirty on foot because you have to detour around canyons."

"It seemed to me an awful long way to walk if

you don't have to," Chee said. "And then there's more questions."

"I think I have the answer to one of them," Leaphorn said. "If you want to believe it."

"It's really a sort of bundle of questions," Chee said. "Jorie went home. So I guess we can presume he was sure the cops wouldn't be coming after him. Didn't have him identified. So forth. So how was he identified? And how did he know he'd been identified? And why didn't the other two members of the crew behave in the same way? Why didn't they go home? And—and so forth."

Leaphorn had extracted a folded paper from his jacket pocket. He opened it, glanced at it.

"That suicide note Jorie left," he said. "It seems to sort of explain some of that."

Chee, who had promised himself never to be surprised by Leaphorn again, was surprised. Had the Legendary Lieutenant just walked off with the suicide note? Surely the FBI wouldn't have given Leaphorn a copy. Chee tried to imagine that and failed. Legendary or not, Leaphorn was now a mere civilian. But the paper Leaphorn was handing him was indeed a suicide note, and the name on the bottom was Jorie's.

"No signature," Chee said.

"It was left on Jorie's computer screen," Leaphorn said. "This is a printout."

Yes, Chee could imagine Leaphorn doing that.

Did the FBI know he'd done it? Highly unlikely. He read through it.

"Wow," Chee said. "This requires some new thinking." He glanced at Professor Bourebonette, who was watching him. Checking his reaction, Chee guessed. She'd read the note, too. Well, why shouldn't she?

"Some things are puzzling," Leaphorn said. "From what Dashee found—just two sets of footprints—Jorie seems to have gotten away from the two somewhere else. Near enough to his home to walk there? But if you look at the map, you see their escape route wouldn't take them there. It would be out of the way. He says in his note they were planning to kill him. That he slipped away. That suggests they stopped somewhere else. But where? And why?"

"Good questions," Chee said.

"I tried to re-create the situation from what little I knew," Leaphorn said. "Jorie, a sort of intellectual. Political idealogue. Fanatic. Doing a robbery to finance his cause. Then it goes sour on him. Unplanned killings. At least unplanned by him. Awareness that his recruits are going to take the loot. There must have been an argument. Or at least an angry quarrel. It must have occurred to Jorie that letting him split off represented a threat to them. How did he manage it?"

"No idea," Chee said.

"Let's say he was still with them when they left the truck. Do you think Dashee might have missed his tracks?"

"They'd stopped in a big flattish place. Mostly covered with old blow dirt. Dashee's good at his job, and it would be hard to miss fresh track in that."

"How about cover? A place to hide?"

"No," Chee said. "A cluster of junipers sort of screened the truck itself from the road. But I didn't see a good place to hide anywhere near. There wasn't one. Certainly not if they were looking for him."

"I presume he was armed," Leaphorn said. "Maybe he warned them away. You know: 'I'm out of here. Let me go or I'm shooting you.'"

"Could have been that," Chee said.

The waitress returned. Leaphorn moved the map to make space for the plates. He looked at Chee. "You had something you wanted to tell me."

"Uh, oh, yeah, I did. About Ironhand. How much do you know about him?"

"Very little."

Chee waited, hoping he'd add to that. From what Dashee had told him Leaphorn knew enough about George Ironhand to have him on the list of names he asked Potts about. But Leaphorn obviously wasn't going to explain that.

"They say a Ute by that same name, about

ninety or so years ago, used to lead a little band of raiders down across the San Juan into our territory. Steal horses, sheep, whatever they could find, kill people, so forth. The Navajos would chase them, but they'd disappear in that rough country along the Nokaito Bench. Maybe into Chinle Wash or Gothic Creek. It started a legend that Ironhand was some sort of Ute witch. He could fly. Our people would see him down in the canyon bottom, and then they'd see him up on the rimrock, with no way to get there. Or sometimes the other way around. Top to bottom. Anyway, Ironhand was never caught."

Leaphorn took a small bite of the hamburger steak he'd ordered, and looked thoughtful.

"Louisa," he said, "have you ever picked up anything like that in your legend collecting?"

"I've read something sort of similar," Professor Bourebonette said. "A man they called Dobby used to raid across the San Juan about the same time. But that was farther west. Down into the Monument Valley area. I think that's more or less on the record. A Navajo named Littleman finally ambushed them in the San Juan Canyon. The way the story goes, he killed Dobby and two of the others. But they were Paiutes, and that happened earlier—in the eighteen nineties, I think it was."

Leaphorn nodded. "I've heard the old folks in

my family talk about that. Littleman was Red Forehead *Dine'*, in my mother's clan."

"It produced a sort of witch story, too," Louisa said. "Dobby could make his men invisible."

Leaphorn put down his fork. "That old Ute you're interviewing at Towaoc tomorrow. Why not see what she remembers about the legendary Ironhand?"

"Why not," Professor Bourebonette said. "It's right down my scholarly alley. And the man you're after is probably Ironhand Junior. Or Ironhand the Second or Third."

She smiled at Chee. "Nothing changes. A century later and you have the same problem in the same canyons."

Chee nodded and returned the smile, but he was thinking there was one big difference. In the 1890s, or 1910s, or whenever it was, the local posse didn't have the FBI city boys telling them how to run their hunt.

FOURTEEN

FROM WHERE JOE Leaphorn sat, he could see the odd shape of Sleeping Ute Mountain out one window, and the Ute Casino about a mile down the slope out of another. If he looked straight ahead, he could watch Louisa and Conrad Becenti, her interpreter. They sat at a card table putting a new tape in their recording machine. Beyond them, on a sofa of bright blue plastic against the wall, sat an immensely old and frail-looking Ute woman named Bashe Lady, her plump and middle-aged granddaughter and a girl about twelve who Leaphorn presumed was a great-granddaughter. Leaphorn himself was perched upon a straight-backed kitchen chair, perched far too long with no end in sight.

Only Bashe Lady and Louisa seemed to be enjoying this session—the old woman obviously glorying in the attention, and Louisa in the role of myth hunter happy with what she was collecting. Leaphorn was fighting off sleep, and the occupants of the sofa had the look of those who had heard all this before, and far too often.

They'd been hearing that Bashe Lady had been born into the Mogche band of the Southern Utes but had married into the Kapot band. With that out of the way, she had used the next hour or so enthusiastically giving Louisa the origin story of both bands. Leaphorn had been interested for thirty minutes or so, but mostly in Professor Bourebonette's technical skills—the questions she chose to direct the interview and the way she made sure she understood what Becenti was telling her. Becenti was part Ute, part Navajo and probably part something else. He had studied mythology with Louisa at Northern Arizona and seemed to still maintain that awe-stricken student-to-teacher attitude.

Leaphorn squirmed into a slightly less uncomfortable position. He watched a truck towing a multisized horse trailer pull into the Ute Casino parking lot, watched its human occupants climb out and head for the gaming tables, noticed a long column of vehicles creeping south on U.S. 666, the cork in this traffic bottle being an overloaded flatbed hauling what seemed to be a well-drilling rig. He found himself wondering if the campaign by Biblical fundamentalists to have the highway number changed from "the mark of the Beast" to something less terrible (turning the signs upside down to make it 999 had been suggested) had any effect on patronage of the casino. Probably not. He shifted from that to trying to decide how the casino management dealt with the problem of chips that surely must have been snatched from roulette tables when the lights went off during the robbery. Probably they had borrowed a different set from another casino. But the discomfort inflicted by the wooden chair seat drove that thought away. He shifted into getting-up position and reached for his empty glass—intending to sneak into the kitchen with it without being rude.

No such luck. The great-granddaughter had been watching him, and apparently watching for her own excuse to escape. She leaped to her feet and confronted him.

"I'll get you some more iced tea," she said, snatched the glass and was gone.

Leaphorn settled himself again, and as he did, the interview got interesting.

". . . and then she said that in those days when the Bloody Knives were coming in all the time and stealing everything and killing people, the Mogches had a young man named Ouraynad, but

people called him Ironhand, or sometimes The
Badger. And he was very good at killing the Bloody
Knives. He would lead our young men down
across the San Juan and they would steal back the
cattle the Bloody Knives had stolen from us."

"OK, Conrad," Louisa said. "Ask her if Ouraynad
was related to Ouray?"

Becenti asked. Bashe Lady responded with a
discourse incomprehensible to Leaphorn, except
for references to Bloody Knives, which was the
Ute nickname for the hated Navajos. Leaphorn
hadn't been bothered by that at first. After all,
the Navajo curing ceremonial used the Utes to
symbolize enemies of the people and the Hopi
phrase for Navajos meant "head breakers," with
the implication his forefathers killed people with
rocks. But now Leaphorn had been hearing the
translator rattle off uncomplimentary remarks
about the *dine'* for about two hours. He was beginning to resent it.

Bashe Lady stopped talking, gave Leaphorn an
inscrutable look and threw out her hands.

"A lot of stuff about the heroism and bravery of
the Great Chief Ouray," Becenti said, "but nothing that's not already published. Bottom line was
she thought this Ironhand was related to Ouray
in some way, but she wasn't sure."

Leaphorn leaned forward and interrupted.

"Could you ask her if this Ironhand had any descendants with the same name?"

Becenti looked at Louisa. Louisa looked at Leaphorn, frowning. "Later," she said. "I don't want to break up her line of thought." And to Becenti: "Ask her if this hero Ironhand had any magical powers. Was he a witch? Anything mystical?"

Becenti asked, with Bashe Lady grinning at him. The grin turned into a cackling laugh, which turned into a discourse, punctuated by more laughter and hand gestures.

"She says they heard the Navajos (Becenti had stopped translating that into Bloody Knives in deference to Leaphorn sitting behind him) were fooled so often by Ironhand that they began believing he was like one of their witches—like a Skinwalker who could change himself into an owl and fly, or a dog and run under the bushes. She said they would hear stories the Navajos told about how he could jump from the bottom of the canyon up to the rim, and then jump down again. But she said the Mogche people knew he was just a man. Just a lot smarter than the Navajos who hunted him. About then they started calling him Badger. Because of the way he fooled the Navajos."

Leaphorn leaned forward into the silence which followed that, and began: "Ask her if this guy had a son."

Louisa looked over her shoulder at him, and said, "Patience. We'll get to that." But then she shrugged and turned back to Becenti.

"Ask her if Ironhand had any children."

He had several, both sons and daughters, Bashe Lady said. Two wives, one a Kapot Ute and the other a Paiute woman. While Becenti was translating that, she burst into enthusiastic discourse again, with more laughter and gestures. Becenti listened, and translated.

"She said he took this Paiute woman when he was old, after his first wife died, and she was the daughter of a Paiute they called Dobby. And Dobby was like Ironhand himself. He killed many Navajos, and they couldn't catch him either. And Ironhand, even when he was an old, old man, had a son by this Paiute woman, and this son became a hero, too."

Louisa glanced back at Leaphorn, looked at Becenti, said, "Ask her what he did to become a hero."

Bashe Lady talked. Becenti listened, inserted a brief question, listened again.

"He was in the war. He was one of the soldiers who wore the green hats. She said he shot a lot of men and got shot twice himself, and they gave him medals and ribbons," Becenti said. "I asked which war. She said she didn't know, but he came home about when they were drilling the new oil wells in the Aneth field. So it must have been Vietnam."

During all this, Great-Granddaughter emerged from the kitchen and handed Leaphorn his renewed glass of iced tea—devoid now of ice cubes. What Bashe Lady had been saying had brought Granddaughter out of lethargy. She listened intently to Becenti's translation, leaned forward. "He was in the army," she said. "In the Special Services, and they put him on the Cambodian border with the hill tribes. The Montagnards. And then they sent him over into Cambodia." She laughed. "He said he wasn't supposed to talk about that."

She paused, looking embarrassed by her interruption. Leaphorn took advantage of the silence. Granddaughter obviously knew a lot about this younger version of Ironhand. He put aside his manners and interjected himself into the program.

"What did he do in the army? Was he some sort of specialist?"

"He was a sniper," she told Leaphorn. "They gave him the Silver Star decoration for shooting fifty-three of the enemy soldiers, and then he was shot, so he got the Purple Heart, too."

"Fifty-three," Leaphorn said, thinking this had to be George Ironhand of the casino robbery, thinking he would hate to be prowling the canyons looking for him.

"Do you know where he lives?"

Granddaughter's expression suggested she didn't like this question. She studied Leaphorn, shook her head.

Becenti glanced back at him, said something to Bashe Lady. She responded with a few words and a couple of hand gestures. In brief she said Ironhand raised cattle at a place north of Montezuma Creek—approximately the same location Leaphorn had been given by Potts and had seen in Jorie's suicide note.

Leaphorn interrupted again.

"Louisa, could you ask her if anyone knows how the first Ironhand got away from the Navajos?"

Becenti was getting caught up in this, too. He didn't wait for approval. He asked. Bashe Lady laughed, answered, and laughed again. Becenti shrugged.

"She said the Navajos thought he got away like a bird, but he got away like a badger."

About then Granddaughter said something in rapid Ute to Bashe Lady, and Bashe Lady looked angry, and then abashed, and decided she knew absolutely nothing more about Ironhand.

When the interview was over and they were heading back toward Shiprock, Louisa wanted to talk about Ironhand Junior, as she had begun calling him. The session had gone well, she said.

A lot of it was what had already been collected about Ute mythology, religion and customs. But some of it, as she put it, "cast some light on how the myths of preliterate cultures evolve with generational changes." And the information about Ironhand was interesting.

Having said that, she glanced at Leaphorn and caught him grinning.

"What?" she said, sounding suspicious.

The grin evolved into a chuckle. "No offense, but when you talk like that it takes me right back to Tempe, Arizona, and sleepy afternoons in the poorly air-conditioned classrooms of Arizona State, and the voices of my professors of anthropology."

"Well," she said, "that's what I am." But she laughed, too. "I guess it gets to be a habit. And it's getting even worse. Postmodernism is in the saddle now, with its own jargon. Anyway, Bashe Lady was a good source. If nothing else, it shows that hostility toward you Bloody Knives still lingers on like Serb versus Croat."

"Except these days we're far too civilized to be killing one another. We marry back and forth, buy each other's used cars, and the only time we invade them it's to try to beat their slot machines."

"OK, I surrender."

But Leaphorn was still a bit chafed from a long

day listening to his people described as brutal invaders. "And as you know very well, Professor, the Utes were the aggressors. They're Shoshoneans. Warriors off the Great Plains moving in on us peaceful Athabascan farmers and shepherds."

"Peaceful shepherds who stole their sheep from who?" Louisa said. "Or is it whom? Anyway, I'm trying to calculate the chronology of this second Ironhand. Wouldn't he be too old now to be the bandit everyone is looking for?"

"Maybe not," Leaphorn said. "The first one would have been operating as late as 1910, which is when we started getting some fairly serious law and order out here. She said the current Ironhand was a child of his old age. Let's say Junior was born in the early forties. That's biologically possible, and that would have him the right age to be in the Vietnam War."

"I guess so. From what she said about him, if I was one of those guys out there trying to find him, I'd be hoping that I wouldn't."

Leaphorn nodded. He wondered how much the FBI knew about Ironhand. And if they did know, how much they had passed along to the locals. He thought about what Bashe Lady had said about how the original Ironhand had eluded the Navajos hunting him. Not like a bird, but like a badger. Badgers escaped when they didn't just stand and fight by diving into their tunnel. Badger tunnels had an exit as well as an entrance. When the hunting ground was canyon country and coal-mining country, that was an interesting thought.

FIFTEEN

ON THE MAPS drawn by geographers it's labeled the Colorado Plateau, with its eighty-five million acres sprawling across Arizona, Colorado, New Mexico and Utah. It is larger than any of those states; mostly high and dry and cut by countless canyons eroded eons ago when the glaciers were melting and the rain didn't stop for many thousand years. The few people who live on it call it the Four Corners, the High Dry, Canyon Land, Slick Rock Country, the Big Empty. Once a writer in more poetic times called it the Land of Room Enough and Time.

This hot afternoon, Sergeant Jim Chee of the Navajo Tribal Police had other names for it, all uncomplimentary and some, after he'd slid into a growth of thistles, downright obscene. He'd spent the day with Officer Jackson Nez, prowling cautiously along the bottom of one of those canyons, perspiring profusely under FBI-issued body armor, carrying an electronic satellite location finder and an infrared body-heat-detecting device and a scoped rifle. What weighed Chee down even more than all that was the confident knowledge that he and Officer Nez were wasting their time.

"It's not a total waste of time," Officer Nez said, "because when the federals can mark off enough of these canyons as searched, they can declare those guys dead and call this off."

"Don't count on it," Chee said.

"Or the perps see us coming and shoot us, and the feds watch for the buzzards, and when they find our bodies, they get their forensic teams in here, and do the match to decide where the shots came from, and then they find the bad guys."

"That makes me feel a little better," Chee said. "Nice to be working with an optimist."

Nez was sitting on a shaded sandstone slab with his body armor serving as a seat cushion while he was saying this. He was grinning, enjoying his own humor. Chee was standing on the sandy bottom of Gothic Creek, body armor on, tinkering with the location finder. Here, away from the cliffs, it was supposed to be in direct contact with the satellite and its exact longitude/latitude numbers would appear on its tiny screen.

Sometimes, including now, they did. Chee pushed the send switch, read the numbers into the built-in mike, shut the gadget off and looked at his watch.

"Let's go home," he said. "Unless you enjoy piling on a lot more overtime."

"I could use the money," Nez said.

Chee laughed. "Maybe they'll add it to your retirement check. We're still trying to collect our overtime for the Great Canyon Climbing Marathon of '98. Let's get out of here before it gets dark."

They managed that, but by the time Chee reached Bluff and his room at the Recapture Lodge, the stars were out. He was tired and dirty. He took off his boots, socks, shirt and trousers, flopped onto the bed, and unwrapped the ham-and-cheese sandwich he'd bought at the filling station across the highway. He'd rest a little, he'd take a shower, he'd hit the sack and sleep, sleep, sleep. He would not think about this manhunt, or about Janet Pete, or about anything else. He wouldn't think about Bernie Manuelito, either. He would set the alarm clock for 6 A.M. and sleep. He took a bite of the sandwich. Delicious. He had another sandwich in the sack. Should have bought a couple more for breakfast. He finished chewing, swallowed, yawned hugely, prepared for a second bite.

From the door the sound: *tap, tap, tap, tap.*

Chee lay still, sandwich raised, staring at the door. *Maybe a mistake*, he thought. *Maybe they will go away.*

Tap, tap, tap, followed by: "Jim. You home?"

The voice of the Legendary Lieutenant.

Chee rewrapped the sandwich, put it on the bedside table, sighed, limped over and opened the door.

Leaphorn stood there, looking apologetic, and beside him was the Woman Professor. She was smiling at him.

"Oops," Chee said, stepping out of her line of vision and reaching for his pants. "Sorry. Let me get some clothes on."

While he was doing that, Leaphorn was apologizing, saying they'd only be a minute. Chee waved them toward the room's two chairs, and sat on the bed.

"You look exhausted," the professor said. "The policewoman at your roadblock said you'd probably been searching in one of the canyons all day. But Joe learned something he felt you needed to know." She gave Chee a wry smile. "I told him you probably already knew it."

"Better safe than sorry," Chee said, and looked at Leaphorn, who was sitting uneasily on the edge of his chair.

"Just a couple of things about this George Ironhand," Leaphorn said. "I guess you knew he was a Vietnam veteran, but we heard today he was a Green Beret. Heard he was a sniper, won a Silver Star. Supposed to have shot fifty-three North Viet soldiers over in Cambodia."

Leaphorn stopped.

Chee thought about that for a moment.

"Fifty-three," he said finally. "I appreciate your telling me. I think if the FBI had let us in on that little secret, Officer Nez would have kept his body armor on in the canyon."

"I imagine the FBI would know this man was a veteran," Leaphorn said. "They're pretty thorough in checking records. But they might not know about the rest of it. To know that, they'd have to turn up the business about him getting decorated."

"Or pass it along if they did," Chee said, his voice now sounding more angry than tired. "We might leak it to the press; the feds wouldn't want the public to know we're chasing a certified official war hero."

"Well," Leaphorn said, "they probably didn't pick up the sniper bit. Army records would just show he received the decoration for something general. Risking his life beyond the call of duty. Something like that."

"OK," Chee said. "I guess I wasn't being fair."

"At least, though," said the professor, "I'd think

they should have told you he was a combat veteran."

"Me, too," Chee said. "But I guess nobody's perfect. I know we weren't today. All we got was a lot of exercise."

"No tracks?"

Chee waved his hands.

"Lots of tracks. Coyotes, goats, rabbits, lizards, snakes, variety of birds every place there was a seep," Chee said. "But no sign of humans. We even picked up what might have been puma tracks. Either that or an oversize big-footed bobcat. One sign of porcupine, rodents galore, from kangaroo rats, to deer mice, to prairie dogs."

"Could you rule out humans?"

"Not really," Chee said. "Too much slick rock. We didn't find a single place in maybe five miles we covered where anybody careful couldn't find rocks to walk on."

"So the hunt goes nowhere," Leaphorn said. "I guess until someone comes up with a better reason for leaving that escape vehicle where it was left."

"You mean better than running down into Gothic Creek to hide?" Chee laughed. "Well, I guess that was better than the first idea. Thinking they trotted over to the Timms place to fly away in that old airplane of his." Chee paused. "Wait a minute. You said you had two things to tell me, Lieutenant. What's the second one. Do you have a better idea?"

Leaphorn looked a bit embarrassed, shook his head.

"Not really," he said. "Just more stuff about George Ironhand. Maybe it might mean something." He glanced at Louisa. "Where do I start?"

"At the beginning," Louisa said. "First tell him about the original Ironhand."

So he recounted the deeds of the legendary Ute hero/bandit, the futile efforts of the Navajos to hunt him down, describing Bashe Lady's account of how those hunting him thought he might be a witch because he seemed able to disappear from a canyon bottom and reappear magically on its rim.

"She said the Navajos thought he escaped like a bird, but actually he escaped like a badger." Leaphorn paused with that, watching for Chee's reaction.

Chee was rubbing his chin, thinking.

"Like a badger," Chee said. "Or a prairie dog. In one hole and out another. Did she give you any hint of where this was happening? Name a canyon, anything like that?"

"None," Leaphorn said.

"Do you think she knows?"

"Probably. At very least, I think she has a pretty good general idea. She knew a lot more than she was willing to tell us about that."

Professor Bourebonette was smiling. "She didn't show any signs of affection for you Navajos. You 'Bloody Knives.' I think that after about four hours of that, she was getting under Joe's skin a little. Right, Joe? Arousing your competitive, nationalistic macho instincts, maybe?"

Leaphorn produced a reluctant chuckle. "OK," he said. "I plead guilty. I was imagining Bashe Lady in one of those John-Wayne-type movies. Tepees everywhere, paint ponies standing around, dogs, cooking fires, young guys with Italian faces and Cheyenne war paint running around yipping and thumping drums, and there's Bashe Lady with a bloody knife in her hand torturing some tied-up prisoners. And I'm thinking of how it actually was in 1863, when these Utes teamed up with the U.S. Army, and the Hispanos and the Pueblo tribes and came howling down on us and—"

Professor Bourebonette held up her hand.

Leaphorn cut that off, made a wry face and a dismissing gesture. "Sorry," he said. "The old lady got on my nerves. And I'll have to admit I'd love to see the Navajo Tribal Police catch this new version of Ironhand and lock him up."

"The point of all this is that the George Ironhand you're looking for is probably the son of the original version," Professor Bourebonette said. "The first one took a new wife when he was old.

The right time span for this guy. Right age to be in the Vietnam War."

Chee nodded. "So the man we're looking for would likely know how his daddy did the badger escape trick. And where he did it." He looked at Leaphorn. "Do you have any ideas about that?"

"Well, I was going to ask you if you had found any mine shafts down in Gothic Creek Canyon."

"We saw several little coal digs. What they call dog holes. None of them went in more than a few yards. Just people digging out a few sacks to get them through the winter. That creek cuts through coal seams in a lot of places, some of them pretty thick. But we didn't see anything that looked like commercial mining."

"Maybe Ironhand has himself a hidden route up some narrow side gulch," Leaphorn said. "From the way the old woman told the story there just had to be a quick way to get up and down the canyon wall. Did you see any little narrow cuts like that? Maybe even a crack a man could climb?"

"Not in the section we covered," Chee said. "Maybe we'll find one farther down toward the San Juan Canyon."

"If they had a secret hidey-hole, I think you'd find it not too far from where they left the truck. They'd be carrying a lot. Food and water probably, unless they stocked up in advance. And four hundred and something thousand dollars. From that casino it would be mostly in small bills. That would be a lot of weight. And then weapons. They apparently used assault rifles at the casino. They're heavy."

That triggered another thought in Chee—a worry that had been nagging for attention.

"You mentioned a roadblock on your way in from the Ute Reservation. An NTP block, I think you said. Talking to a policewoman."

"It was one of our patrol cars, but the man sitting in it was wearing a San Juan County deputy uniform. The woman was wearing a Navajo Police uniform. Up here it would probably be one of your people out of Shiprock."

Chee was doing a quick inventory of policewomen at Shiprock. There weren't many. "How old?" he asked. "How big?"

Leaphorn knew exactly what he was asking.

"I've only seen her a time or two," he said. "But I think it was Bernadette Manuelito."

"Son of a bitch," Chee said, voice vehement. "What are they using for brains?" He was pulling on his socks. "What the devil does she know about staying alive at a roadblock?"

SIXTEEN

THE ROADBLOCK AS Leaphorn described it was on Utah 163 about halfway between Recapture Creek and the Montezuma Creek Bridge. A sensible place to put it, Chee thought, since a fugitive who spotted it would have no side trails to detour onto. There was only the brush bosque of the San Juan River to the south and the sheer stone cliffs of McCracken Mesa to the north. What wasn't sensible was assigning Bernie to such dangerous duty. That was insane. Bernie would be working backup, surely. Even so, this would be a three-unit block at best. Whoever they had would be up against men who had already proved their willingness to kill and their ability to do it. They'd used an automatic rifle at the casino, and a rumor was afloat that they also had night-vision scopes missing from a Utah National Guard armory.

Chee imagined a bloody scene and drove the first eight miles of his trip much faster than the rules allowed. Then, abruptly, he slowed. A belated thought worked its way through his anger. What was he going to say when he got there? What would he say to the officer in charge? It would probably be a Utah state cop, or a San Juan County deputy. He tried to imagine the conversation. He'd introduce himself as NTP out of Shiprock, chat about the weather maybe, discuss the manhunt a minute or two. Then what? They'd want to know what he wanted. He'd tell 'em he didn't think Bernie had any roadblock training.

Down the slope, Chee's headlights illuminated a red REDUCE SPEED sign.

Then what would they say? Chee took his foot off the gas pedal, let the car roll, imagining a tough-looking Utah cop grinning at him, saying, "She's your lady? Well, then, we'll take good care of her for you." And a deputy sheriff standing behind him, chuckling. An even more dreadful thought emerged. The next step. They'd tell Bernie she had to stay in her car, run and hide anytime a stop seemed imminent. Bernie would be outraged, furious, terminally resentful. And justifiably so.

The car was rolling slowly now. Chee pulled it off onto the shoulder, slammed it into reverse, made a pursuit turn, and headed back toward Bluff, giving his idea of saving Officer Bernadette Manuelito more thought.

That thought was quickly interrupted. The sound of a siren in his ear, the blinking warning light atop a Utah State Police car reflecting off his rearview mirror. Chee grunted out the Navajo version of an expletive, slammed himself on the forehead with a free hand, and angled his car off on the shoulder. Of course. He'd done exactly what one does to trigger pursuit from every road-block from Argentina to Zanzibar. He put on the parking brake, extracted his NTP identification, turned on the overhead light, did everything he could think of to make it easier for whichever cop would show up at his driver-side window.

He'd guessed right for once. It proved to be a Utah State Policeman.

He shined his flash on Chee, looked at the iden-tification Chee was holding out, and said, "Out of the car, please," and stepped back.

Chee opened the door and got out.

"Face the car please, and put your hands on the roof."

Chee did so, happy he'd left his belt and holster on the motel bed, and was patted down.

"OK," the State Policeman said.

And then another voice, Bernie's voice, saying:

"That's Sergeant Chee. Jim, what are you doing here?"

And Chee stood there, still leaning against the car, grimacing, wondering if there was any way things could possibly get any worse.

SEVENTEEN

THE EASTERN SKY was glowing pink and red over
the bluffs that gave Bluff, Utah, its name when
Officer Jim Chee climbed into his patrol car. He
inserted the key, started the engine, did what all
empty-country drivers habitually do: he checked
the fuel gauge. The needle hovered between half
and quarter full. Plenty to get back to the rendez-
vous point on Casa Del Eco Mesa, where Nez and
he were scheduled to resume the search of their
canyon. But not enough to feel comfortable when
you're going a long way from paved road and service stations. He glanced at his watch, pulled out
of the Recapture Lodge lot onto U.S. 163. The
Chevron station-diner he'd pass should be open
about now. He'd stop, fill the tank, buy a few
emergency-ration candy bars to share with Nez

and continue, not thinking about how foolish he'd looked last night.

Good. The station must be open. He couldn't see whether the lights were on, but a pickup was driving away. Chee stopped by the pumps, got out. A man was sitting on the gravel beside the station's door, back against the wall. If Chee had numbered the drunks he'd dealt with since he joined the Navajo Tribal Police, this one would be about 999. He stepped out of the car, wondering what the station operator was doing, and gave the drunk a closer look.

Blood was trickling down the man's forehead. Chee squatted beside him. The man looked about sixty, hair graying, wearing a khaki shirt with LEROY DELL embroidered on it. The man was breathing heavily. The blood came from an abrasion cut over his right eye. Chee started for the car to radio this in and get an ambulance. Get a pursuit started.

"What? What are you doing? Oh!"

Chee spun around. The man was staring at him, eyes wild, getting up.

"What happened?" the man asked. "Where is he? Did he get away?"

Chee helped him to his feet. "You tell me who hit you," he said. "I'll radio it in and get you an ambulance and we'll see if we can catch him."

"The son of a bitch," the man said. He waved his hands. "Look at the mess he made."

On the other side of the entrance, under a sign reading REST ROOMS CUSTOMERS ONLY, a garbage can lay on its side, surrounded by a scattering of cans, bottles, newspapers, sacks, crumpled napkins—all those things people discard at service stations. Nearby, a newspaper-vending machine was on its back.

"Who was he?" Chee said. "I want to call it in. Give us a better chance to catch him."

"I don't know him," the man said. "He was a big Indian-looking guy. Navajo probably, or maybe a Ute. Tall. Maybe middle-aged, or so."

"Driving a blue pickup truck?"

"I didn't see the truck. Didn't notice it."

"Did he have a weapon?"

"That's what he hit me with. A pistol."

"OK," Chee said. "Why don't you go in and sit down. I'll get the police on it."

The dispatcher sounded sleepy until the pistol was mentioned.

"Call him armed and dangerous," Chee suggested. "You might mention this is in the area we're hunting the Ute Casino perps."

The dispatcher chuckled. "Those the perps the feds said were long gone. Flown away?"

"Don't we wish," Chee replied, and went back

into the station to find out just what had happened.

Leroy Dell was sitting behind the cash register, holding his head.

"They'll be sending an ambulance," Chee said.

"Down from Blanding. About twenty-five miles from the clinic, and twenty-five back," Dell said. He groaned and grimaced and described to Chee what had happened. When he was walking from his house up behind the station to open the place he'd heard a sort of a crashing sound. He'd hurried around the corner and seen a man going through the trash. He had shouted at him, and the man had said he just wanted to get some old newspapers.

"Just newspapers?"

"That's what he said. And I said, 'Well you're going to have to clean up the mess, too.' And then I noticed the vending machine was turned over and went to look at that and I saw he'd broken into that. And I turned around and said he was going to have to pay for that and he had this gun in his hand and he hit me."

"What kind of gun?"

"Pistol. I don't know what kind. It wasn't a revolver."

"Anything missing?"

"I don't know," Dell said, grimacing again.

"Tell the truth, I don't give a damn. I've got a hell of a headache. You take a look if you want to."

Chee looked. He opened the cash-register drawers.

"Empty."

"I take the money home at night," Dell said.

"You better call somebody to come down here and look after you," Chee said. "I'm going to get myself some gas and see if I can find that pickup truck."

Finding the truck occupied much of the day. A Bureau of Indian Affairs cop sent over from the Jicarilla Apache Reservation in New Mexico spotted it at the Aneth Oil Field about sundown. It was stuck in the sand of an arroyo bottom off an abandoned road. South of Montezuma Creek. West of Highway 35. Back on the emptiness of Casa Del Eco Mesa. Back within easy walking range of Gothic Canyon, or Desert Creek Canyon, or anyplace else for a man burdened only by an old newspaper.

It was farther, however, than Sergeant Jim Chee could have walked that evening. Chee had sprained his left ankle climbing down a rocky slope while on this fruitless hunt. It had been one of those no-brainer accidents. He'd put his weight on a protruding slab of sandstone that looked solid but wasn't. Then, instead of facing the inevitability of gravity and taking the tumble with a roll in the rocks, he'd tried to save his dignity, made an off-balance jump and landed wrong. That hurt, and it hurt even worse to require help from a deputy sheriff and an FBI agent to haul him back to his car.

EIGHTEEN

THE VOICE ON the telephone was Captain Largo's, with no words wasted.

Chee said, "No sir, I can't put any weight on it yet," listened a few moments, said, "Yes sir," listened again, another "Yes sir," and clicked off. Total result: Largo wanted to know when Chee could resume his canyon-combing duties, preferably immediately; Largo instructed him to fill out an injury report form, and Largo had already sent somebody down to his trailer with it. It should include name, phone number, etc., of the physician who had X-rayed the ankle. Chee should do this immediately and send the report right back. Largo was shorthanded, and Chee should not waste the messenger's time with a lot of conversation.

Chee adjusted the ice pack. He tried to think

of the word, in either Navajo or English, to describe the color the swelling had turned and settled on "plum-colored." He considered whether he should resent the lack of either sympathy or confidence the captain's call had indicated. About the time he'd decided to pass that off as part of Largo's natural-born grumpiness, the messenger arrived.

"Come on in," Chee said, and Officer Bernadette Manuelito stepped in, in full uniform and looking neater than usual.

"Wow," she said. "Look at that ankle." She made a wry face. "I'll bet it hurts."

"Right," Chee said.

"You're lucky you didn't get shot," she said, her tone disapproving. "Barging right in like that."

"I didn't 'barge right in.' I drove up to get some gasoline. I noticed a pickup driving away. Then I saw the victim sitting by the wall. And weren't you supposed to bring me a report to fill in and then rush right back to the captain with it, with no time wasted talking?"

"I still think you were lucky," Manuelito said. "You're a fine one to be thinking I wasn't competent to work on a roadblock."

Chee was conscious of his face flushing. He looked at Bernie, found her expression odd but inscrutable—at least to him.

"Where'd you hear that?"

"Professor Bourebonette told me."

"I don't believe it," Chee said. "When did she say that? And why would she say anything like that?"

"At the roadblock. She and Lieutenant Leaphorn came through about an hour or so after you—" Bernie hesitated, seeking a way to describe Chee's arrival. "After you were there. They stopped and talked a while. That's when she said it. She asked me if you had come by, and I said yes, and she asked me what you'd said, and I said nothing much. And she acted surprised, and I asked why, and she said you'd gotten all angry and excited when they told you they'd seen me at the road-block and ran right out and drove away."

Chee was still trying to read her expression. Was it fond, or amused? Or both.

"I didn't say you were incompetent."

Officer Manuelito said, "Well, OK," and shrugged.

"I just thought it was too dangerous. Those guys had already shot two cops, and shot at another one, and the Ironhand guy, he'd killed a lot more in Vietnam."

"Well, thanks then." Manuelito's expression was easy to read now. She was smiling at him.

"The captain said for you to rush that report right back to him," Chee said, and held out his hand.

She gave it to him, secured to a clipboard with a pen dangling.

"Which one was it? Ironhand or Baker?"

"A tall, middle-aged Indian," Chee said. "Sounds like Ironhand."

"And he just took newspapers? Like the radio said this morning?"

Chee was trying to fill in the form with the clipboard balanced on his right knee. "Apparently. The victim didn't think anything else was missing. But then he was still pretty stunned."

"I think you should call Lieutenant Leaphorn," Manuelito said. "It sounds awfully funny."

Chee looked up at her. "Why?"

"Because, you know, running that risk just to get a newspaper."

"I meant why call Leaphorn?"

"Well, you know, I think he'd be interested. At the roadblock he told us we should be extra careful because he guessed it would be about now those guys, if they were hiding in the canyons, about now they'd be making their move. And the deputy I was working with said he thought they'd be more likely to lie low until everybody got tired of looking before they made a run, and the lieutenant said, maybe so, but their radio was broken. They'd wouldn't know what was going on. They'd be getting desperate to know something."

"He said that?" Chee said, sounding incredulous. "About making their move now. How the devil could Leaphorn have guessed?" Manuelito shrugged.

"And that's why you think I should call him?"

Now it was Bernie's turn to look slightly embarrassed. She hesitated. "I like him," she said. "And he likes you. And I think he's a very lonely man, and—"

The buzz of the telephone cut her off. Captain Largo again.

"What the hell are you and Manuelito doing?" Largo said. "Get her back up here with that report."

"She just left a minute ago," Chee said. He clicked off, filled in the last space, signed the form, handed it to her. Leaphorn liked him? Nobody had ever suggested that before. He'd never even thought of it. Of Leaphorn liking anyone, for that matter. Leaphorn was— Well, he was just Leaphorn.

"You know, Bernie," he said. "I think I will call the lieutenant. I'd like to know what he's thinking."

NINETEEN

HAVING RESIGNED HIMSELF to more long hours spent listening to elderly Utes recounting their tribal mythology, Joe Leaphorn was reaching for his cap when the phone rang.

"Hello," he said, sounding glum even to himself.

The voice was Jim Chee's. Leaphorn brightened.

"Lieutenant, if you have a minute or two, I'd like to fill you in on what happened at the Chevron station in Bluff yesterday. Have you heard about that? I'd like to find out what you think about it."

"I have time," Leaphorn said. "But all I know is what I got on the television news. A man shows up at the station around opening time. He knocks out the operator and drives off in a previously stolen pickup truck. The FBI presumes the man was one of the casino bandits. The newscaster said a Navajo Tribal Policeman was at the station buying gas when it happened, but the robber escaped. Is that about it?"

A moment of silence. "Well, I was the one buying the gas," Chee said, sounding somewhat defensive, "but I wasn't there until it had already happened. The perp was driving off as I drove up. But what's interesting is that all the man wanted was a newspaper. He took one from the rack, and when the operator got there and found him digging through the trash barrel, he said he was just hunting a newspaper.

Now it was Leaphorn's turn for a moment of silence.

"Just a newspaper," he said. "Just that. And he hadn't taken anything from inside the station. Food, cigarettes, anything like that?"

"The station was still locked up. I thought maybe the guy had taken the operator's keys after he hit him. Got in, looted the place, and then relocked it—silly as that sounds—but apparently not."

"Well now," Leaphorn said, sounding thoughtful. "He just wanted a newspaper out of the rack."

"Or maybe another one. From what he'd scattered around out of the trash can, he was hunting something there, and he told the operator he was after a newspaper. I was guessing he wanted an older edition. One reporting earlier stuff about the manhunt."

"Sounds reasonable. Where are you calling from?"

"My place in Shiprock. I hurt my ankle yesterday hunting the newspaper bandit. I took a fall, and I'm homebound until I get the swelling down. I called your place in Window Rock and got another of those messages you leave on your answering machine. That's a good idea."

"Just a minute," Leaphorn said. He put his hand over the telephone and looked at Louisa, who was standing in the doorway, tape-recorder case over her shoulder, purse in hand, waiting and looking interested.

"It's Jim Chee at Shiprock," Leaphorn said. "You know that Chevron station robbery we were talking about. Chee said the only thing the man wanted was newspapers. Remember what I was saying about that broken radio—"

"That sounds strange," Louisa said. "And look, unless you really want to come along and listen to this mythology cross-examination, why don't you drive over to Shiprock and talk to Chee? I'll ride with Mr. Becenti."

That was exactly the way Emma would have reacted, Leaphorn thought. And he noticed with a sort of joy that he could make such a comparison now without feeling guilty about it.

The door of Chee's little house trailer was standing open as Leaphorn drove up, and he heard his "come on in" shout as he closed the door of his pickup. Chee was sitting beside the table, his left foot propped on a pillow on his bunk. As they exchanged the required greetings, the words of sympathy, the required disclaimer and disclaimer response, Leaphorn noticed the table was bare except for a copy of the Indian Country Map, unfolded to the Four Corners canyon country.

"I see you're ready for work," he said, tapping the map.

"My uncle used to tell me to use my head to save my heels," Chee said. "Since I have to save my ankle today, I'll have to think instead."

Leaphorn sat. "What have you come up with?"

"Nothing but confusion," Chee said. "I was hoping you could explain it all to me."

"It's as if we have a jigsaw puzzle with a couple of the central pieces missing," Leaphorn said. "But driving over from Farmington I began thinking how two of the pieces fit."

"The broken radio producing the need to get a paper to find out what the devil has been going on," Chee said. "Right?"

"Right. And that can tell us something."

Chee frowned. "Like they don't have another radio? Or any other access to news? Or something more than that?"

Leaphorn smiled. "I have an advantage in this situation, being able to sit by a telephone and tap into the retired-cops circuit while you're out working."

Chee leaned forward and readjusted his ice pack, engulfed in déjà vu—a sort of numb feeling of intellectual inadequacy. He'd heard this sort of preamble from Leaphorn often enough before to know where it led. It was the Legendary Lieutenant's way of leading into some disclosure without making Chee, the green kid who'd been assigned to be his gofer, feel more stupid than necessary. "To tell the truth, all this tells me is that these guys, without their radio, got desperate to find out what the devil was going on. They had to find out whether or not it was time to run."

"Exactly," Leaphorn said. "That's my conclusion, too. But let me add a little bit of information that wasn't available to you. I think I told you I might call Jay Kennedy to see if he could tell us what the FBI lab learned about that radio. Jay called back yesterday. He said his buddy back there told him the radio had been put out of commission deliberately."

Chee lost interest in realigning the ice pack.

He stared at Leaphorn. Leaphorn said he'd asked Kennedy to "tell us."

"On purpose?" Chee said. "Why would they do that? Or, wait a minute. Let me restate that question. Make it which one did it, and why? And how could the Bureau determine it was done deliberately?"

"Never underestimate the Bureau's laboratory people. They took the radio apart to see if they could pick up any prints. The sort someone might leave changing batteries, or whatever. They noticed that a couple of the wire connections inside had been pried apart with something sharp. Knife point maybe."

Chee thought for a moment. "Fingerprints," he said. "Did they find any?" If they had, they would be Jorie's. Jorie, knowing he was being betrayed, doing a vengeful act of sabotage.

"Some partials," Leaphorn said. "But they belonged to nobody they had any record of."

Chee thought about that, noticed that Leaphorn was watching him, waiting his reaction. Whose prints would the FBI have on record? Jorie's of course, since they had his body. Perhaps Ironhand's, if they printed servicemen during the Vietnam War. Probably Baker's. He'd been arrested on minor stuff more than once.

"It could still be Jorie who sabotaged the radio,"

Chee said. "He could have had on gloves, used a handkerchief, been very careful with his knife."

Leaphorn nodded, smiling.

He's happy I thought it through, Chee thought. *Maybe Bernie was right. Maybe Leaphorn does like me.*

"I'd guess the prints don't mean much," Leaphorn said. "They'll belong to some clerk at a Radio Shack who put the battery in. I was thinking about Jorie, too. He still looks like the logical bet."

"He certainly had a motive. We have to presume he had access to the radio after he knew what they were planning."

Leaphorn nodded. "If he had decided to turn them in, he wouldn't want them to know the cops had them identified. Wouldn't want them to hear anything on the radio."

Chee nodded.

"There's a problem with that, though."

"Yeah," Chee said, wondering which problem Leaphorn saw. "Certainly a lot of unanswered questions left."

"Jorie must have thought he knew what he was talking about when he told the police in that suicide note where to find them. At their homes, he said, or that place up north. FBI went to get them, and they weren't there. Why not?" He looked at Chee to see if he would volunteer an answer.

"They didn't trust him," Chee said.

Leaphorn nodded. "They wouldn't. Not when they were double-crossing him." He tapped the map. "And next, why did they come up on this mesa?"

"I have two answers to that. Take your pick. One, I think they may have had a second escape vehicle hidden away someplace not far from where they ditched the pickup. Cowboy said they could find no trace of it, no tracks. Nothing. But in this country they could hide the tracks, knowing they had to, and taking their time to do it right."

Leaphorn acknowledged this with the barest hint of a nod.

"The second idea goes back to what you learned about Ironhand. He knew where his daddy hid during his career. How he managed his magical, mystical escapes. So I say that hiding place is around there someplace. The perps stocked it with food and water. And that's where they intend to hide until it's safe to make a run for it. That's why they drove the truck over the rock—ripped out the oil pan to make it appear to the FBI that they were forced to abandon it there. Then they hiked away to their hidey-hole."

Leaphorn's nod acknowledging this was a bit less languorous.

"But they didn't tell Jorie anything about this. It was their secret. Which means the double cross was planned far in advance of the crime."

"Sure," Chee said.

"I'm thinking of that second choice to look for them Jorie gave the police. That's way up toward Blanding. A long, long way from where they abandoned the pickup."

Chee sighed. "Wouldn't it be wonderful if Cowboy had found three sets of tracks at that damned truck."

Leaphorn laughed. "But let's set that aside for now and get back to your second idea. We'll say Baker and Ironhand had a place arranged to hide out. Jorie had parted company with them somehow before they got there. So Baker and Ironhand leave the truck and start walking. It wouldn't be a long walk because, if we can believe what Jorie said in that note, they must have been carrying a heavy load of paper money. Presuming they hadn't left it somewhere else, and why would they?"

"Heavy? I don't think of paper money as being heavy."

"I was guessing the Ute Casino wouldn't be using many hundred-dollar bills. I guessed a ten-dollar average, and came up with forty-five thousand pieces of paper."

"Be damned," Chee said. "That's a new factor to be thinking about."

"I'm remembering the old Ute lady said the Utes sometimes called the original Ironhand Badger.

She said he'd disappear from the canyon bottom and reappear at the top. Or the other way around. Remember that? She said our people chasing him thought he could fly."

"Yes," Chee said. But he was thinking about a huge problem with the second idea. With both of them, in fact. Jorie. Given what he said in the suicide note about where to find his partners, he must have slipped away from them long before they abandoned the truck. The distances were simply too great. Especially if they were humping almost a hundred pounds of money as well as their weapons. But how could he have slipped away? Probably possible. But then, why would he believe his partners would be going home? Wouldn't he know they'd expect him to betray them?

Leaphorn was pursuing his own line of speculation. "Thinking of badgers got me to thinking of holes in the ground," he said. "Of old coal mines. This part of the world has far more than its share of those. Coal almost everywhere. And then when the uranium boom started in the forties, the geologists remembered how the coal veins were usually mixed with uranium deposits, and they were digging away again."

"Yeah," Chee said. "We noticed three or four old digs when we were looking for tracks down in the Gothic Creek Canyon."

Leaphorn looked very interested in that. "How

deep? Real tunnels, or just places where people were taking a few wagonloads?"

"Nothing serious," Chee said. "Just a place where somebody got a sackful to heat the hogan."

"When the Mormon settlers moved in the middle of the nineteenth century they found the Navajos were already digging a little coal out of exposed seams. So were the Utes. But the Mormons needed a lot more to fire up smelters, so they developed some tunnel mines. Then the Aneth field development came, and there was natural gas to burn. The mines weren't economical any longer. Some of them were filled in, and some of them collapsed. But there must be some around there in one form or another."

"You're thinking they're hiding in a mine. I don't know. Where I grew up near Rough Rock people dug a little coal, but it was all just shallow stuff. We called them dog-hole mines. Nothing anyone could hide in."

"That's over in the Chuska Mountains," Leaphorn said. "Volcanic geology. Over by Gothic Creek Canyon it's mostly formed by sedimentation. Stratum after stratum."

"True."

"An old-timer in Mexican Water—old fella named Mortimer I think it was—told me there used to be a slide cut down the cliff on the south side of the San Juan across from Bluff. From the rimrock all the way down. He said his folks would dig the coal out of seams in the canyon, hoist it to the top, load it into oxcarts and then dump it down the slide into carts down by the river. Then they'd ferry it across on a cable ferry."

Chee was feeling a little less skeptical. "When was that?"

"It was about forty years ago when he told me, I'd guess, but he was talking about his parents when he was a child. I guess it was operating in the 1880s, or thereabouts. I'd like to take a look at that old mine if it still exists."

"You think we could still find it? Maybe locate the wagon tracks and trace them back? Trouble is, wagon tracks tend to get wiped out in a hundred years."

"I think we might find it another way," Leaphorn said. "Did you ever take a look at those notices posted on chapter-house bulletin boards? The Environmental Protection Agency put them up. They have maps on them showing where the EPA is going to be flying its copters back and forth making surveys of old mine sites."

"I've seen them," Chee said. "But they're surveying to map old uranium-mine sites. Trying to locate radioactive dumps."

"Basically, yes. But what the monitors show is spots with high radiation levels. Coal seams out here are often associated with uranium deposits, and the one Mortimer told me about must have been a pretty big operation. I don't have any business in this, but if I did, I'd call the EPA down in Flagstaff and see if they have a mine-waste map for that part of the Reservation."

"I guess I could do that," Chee said, sounding doubtful about it.

"Here's the reason I'd be hopeful," Leaphorn said. "Coal seams out here vary a lot in depth. Some right on the surface, some hundreds of feet down, and all depths between. You couldn't haul it down the canyon bottom to the river. Too rough. Too many barriers. I'm thinking the Mormons must have got tired of hauling it up to the top after digging it, and dug down to the seam from the top of the mesa. They hoisted it to the top with some sort of elevator like they still do in most tunnel mines."

"Which would explain how our Ironhand could fly from bottom to top," Chee said. "How our Badger could have two holes."

He picked up the telephone, dialed information, and asked for the Environmental Protection Agency number in Flagstaff.

TWENTY

ON THE FOURTH call and after the sixth or seventh explanation of what he wanted to various people in various DOE and EPA offices in Las Vegas, Nevada, and Flagstaff, Arizona, Sergeant Jim Chee found himself referred to a New Mexico telephone number and enlightened.

"Call this number in Farmington," the helpful person in Albuquerque said. "That's the project's fixed base. Ask for either the fixed base operator or the project manager." That number took him right back to the Farmington Airport, no more than thirty miles or so from his aching ankle.

"Bob Smith here," the answering voice said.

Chee identified himself, rattled off what he was after. "Are you the project manager?"

"I'm a combination technical guy on the helicopter and driver of the refueling truck," Smith said. "And I'm the wrong guy to talk to for what you want. I'll try to get you switched to P.J. Collins."

"What's his title?"

"It's her," Smith said. "I think you'd call her the chief scientist on this job. Hold on. I'll get her."

P.J. answered the phone by saying, "Yes," in a tone that busy people use. Chee explained again, hurrying it a little.

"Does this involve that casino robbery? Shooting those policemen?"

"Well, yes," Chee said. "We're checking on places they might be hiding. We know there's an old coal mine in Gothic Creek Canyon, abandoned maybe eighty or ninety years ago, and we thought that perhaps—"

"Good thinking," P.J. said. "Especially the 'perhaps' part. That coal up in that part of the world is uraniferous. Well, all coal tends to be a little radioactive, but that area is hotter than most. But that's a lot of years for the radioactive stuff to get washed away, or lose its punch. However, if you can give me a general idea of where the mine might be, I'll tell you if we've surveyed that area. If we have, I can get Jesse to check our maps in the van and see what hot spots showed up. If any."

"Great," Chee said. "We think this mine was dug into the east slope of Gothic Creek Canyon.

It would be somewhere in a ten-mile stretch of the canyon from where it runs into the San Juan southward."

"Well, that's good," P.J. said. "That's on the Navajo Reservation, and that's what our contract covers. The Department of Energy has hired us to help 'em clean up the mess they left hunting uranium. They provide the copters and the pilots, and we provide the technicians."

"Do you think you've surveyed there yet?"

"Possibly today," she said. "We've been up there south of Bluff and Montezuma Creek this week. If they didn't cover that today, they probably will tomorrow."

Chee had been feeling foolish during most of his earlier telephone conversations, his skepticism about this idea reviving. Now he found himself getting excited. P.J. seemed to be taking the notion seriously.

"Can I give you my number? Have you call me back? I'll be reachable tonight and tomorrow and however long it takes."

"Where you calling from?"

"Shiprock."

"The copter will be coming in about an hour or so. Calling it quits for the day and downloading all the data they've collected. Why don't you drive on over and see for yourself?"

Why not, indeed. "I'll be there," he said.

Chee had given up on putting on his left sock, and was easing a sandal on that foot when he heard a vehicle bumping down his access road. It stopped, the west wind blew a puff of dust past his screen door, and a few moments later Officer Bernadette Manuelito appeared. She was carrying what seemed to be a tray covered with a white cloth, holding the cloth against the breeze with one hand, tapping on the screen with the other.

"*Ya'eeh te'h,*" she said. "How's the ankle? Would you like something to eat?"

Chee said he would. But not right now. He had a can't-wait errand to run.

Bernie had been looking at the sandal on his left foot, frowning at it. It was not a pretty sight. She shook her head.

"You can't go anywhere," she said. "You can't drive. What do you think you're doing?" She put the tray on the table.

"It's just over to the Farmington Airport," Chee said. "Of course I can drive. Why not? You use your right foot for the gas pedal and the brake."

"Take off the sandal," Officer Manuelito said. "We'll wrap it up in the bandage again. If you think it can't wait, I'll drive you over there."

Which was, of course, what happened.

The woman who Chee presumed was P.J. turned out to be the same small, slightly sunburned blonde he'd noticed at the helicopter when he'd come to talk to Jim Edgar. She was standing beside the craft holding a black metal box, the box being linked by an insulated cable to the big white pod mounted on the copter's landing skid. When she noticed Chee limping up, her expression was skeptical. *Not surprising*, he thought. He was wearing his worn and wrinkled "stay at home" jeans and a blue T-shirt on which some of the mutton stew Bernie had brought him had splashed when she drove too fast over a bumpy place.

Chee introduced Officer Bernadette Manuelito, who looked uncharacteristically neat and spiffy in her uniform, and himself.

P.J. smiled. "I'm Patti Collins. Just a minute until I get this data unloaded."

Jim Edgar was leaning on the doorframe of his hangar watching them. He held up his hand in salute, shouted, "Heard you found Old Man Timms's airplane," and disappeared back in the direction of his workbench.

P.J. was unjacking the cable. "You got here fast," she said. "Let's take this into the lab and see what we have."

The lab was a standard-looking Winnebago mobile home, its white exterior badly in need of washing but the interior immaculate.

"Have a seat somewhere," P.J. said. She connected her black metal box to an expensive-looking console built into the back of the vehicle and did those incomprehensible things technicians do.

The console made computer sounds. The attached printer began spewing out a roll of paper. P.J. studied it. "Well, now," she said. "I don't know if this is going to help you much, but it's interesting." She detached a couple of feet of paper and laid it on a large scale U.S. Geological Survey map spread across the tabletop where Chee and Bernie were sitting.

"See this," she said, and traced her finger down a tight squiggle of lines on the computer printout. "That coordinates with this." She traced the same fingertip down Gothic Creek on the USGS map.

It was meaningless to Chee. He said, "Oh."

"It shows there's been a distribution of radioactive material downstream from here," P.J. said, tapping her finger on the *h* in Gothic Creek on the map legend.

"Would that suggest the mine waste dump might have been there?" Chee asked. "That would be interesting."

"Yeah," P.J. said, studying the printout again. "Now my problem is whether it's interesting enough to divert the copter a couple of miles tomorrow to get a closer scan."

"It would be a big help to us," Chee said.

"I'll talk to the pilots," P.J. said. "It would just

take another twenty minutes or so. And if it's hot enough, we ought to get it on the map anyway."

"Would there be room for me to go along?"

P.J. looked at him skeptically. "You were limping along on that cane. What's the deal with your ankle?"

"I sprained it," Chee said. "It's just about healed."

She still looked skeptical. "You ridden in a copter before?"

"Twice," Chee said. "I didn't enjoy it either time, but I've got a good stomach for motion sickness."

"I'll let you know," she said. "Give me the number where you'll be tonight. If it's go, I'll call you and tell you where to meet the refueling truck."

TWENTY-ONE

FOR ONCE CHEE came out lucky with the timing. As promised, P.J. had called him. Yes, they would revise their schedule for the next day a bit and divert a few miles to do a follow-up low-level check of the Gothic Creek drainage. He could go along. Everything had been more or less cleared and approved. However, it was one of those "less said the better" affairs. Why run the risk that some big shot far removed from the scene might suspect this rational interpretation of regulations could cause trouble? The most economical and convenient time to do this diversion would be the final flight of the day. Chee should be at the refueling truck at 2:40 P.M., at which time the truck would be at the same place Chee had seen it previously, parked beside the road leading to the Timms place on Casa Del Eco Mesa.

"Thanks," Chee said. "I'll be there waiting."

And he was. He'd gotten down to the office in the morning, caught up on paperwork, handled some chores for Captain Largo, had lunch, bought himself some snack stuff (including an extra apple to offer to Rosner) and headed west for the mesa. By two-fifteen, he and Rosner were sitting in the shade of the truck snacking and watching the copter land. It was the same big white Bell with radiation-sensor pods on its landing skids, and the pilot put it down far enough away to avoid blasting them with dust.

Rosner drove the truck over. He introduced Chee to pilot, copilot and technician, and started refueling.

"P.J. told me something about what you're looking for," the pilot said. "I'm not sure she had it right. Mine opening up on the canyon wall. Is that it?"

The pilot's name was Tom McKissack. He looked a weather-beaten sixty or so, and Chee remembered P.J. had said McKissack was one of those army pilots who'd survived the risky business of rescuing wounded Air Mobile Division grunts from various Vietnam battles. He introduced Chee to the copilot, a younger fellow named Greg DeMoss, another army copter veteran, and to Jesse, who would be doing the technical work. All three looked tired, dusty and not particularly thrilled by this detour.

"Sounds like P.J. had it right," Chee said. "We're trying to locate the mouth of an old Mormon coal mine abandoned back in the 1880s. We think it has a mouth fairly high up the canyon wall. Probably on a shelf of some sort. And then on top, maybe the remains of a tipple structure where they hoisted the coal up and dumped it."

McKissack nodded and looked at the Polaroid camera Chee was carrying. "They tell me those things are a lot better now," he said. He handed Chee a barf bag and a flight helmet, and explained how the intercom system worked.

"You'll be sitting on the right side behind De-Moss, which gives you a great view to the right, but nothing much to the front or the left. So if your mine is on the east side, your best chance to see it will be when we're going north, down the creek toward the river."

"OK," Chee said.

"We normally fly a hundred and fifty feet off the terrain, which means our equipment is scoping a swath three hundred feet wide. Down a canyon it may be lower, but we rarely get closer than fifty feet. Anyway, if you see something interesting, holler. If the situation is right, I can hover a minute so maybe you can get pictures."

McKissack started the rotors. "One more thing," he said, his voice coming through the intercom now. "We've been shot at a few times out here.

Either people think we're the black helicopters the Conspiracy Commandos are taking over the world with, or maybe we're scaring their sheep. Who knows? Are we likely to get shot at in this canyon here?"

Chee considered that a moment and gave an honest answer. He said, "Probably not," and they took off in a chaos of dust, motor noise and rotor thumping.

Later Chee had very few memories of that flight, but the ones he retained were vivid.

The tableland was of multicolored stone, carved into a gigantic labyrinth by canyons, all draining eventually into the narrow green belt of the San Juan bottom. Multiple hundreds of miles of sculptured stone, cut off in the north by the blue-green of the mountains. The slanting afternoon sun outlined it into a pattern of gaudy red sandstone and deep shadows. The voice in Chee's ear saying: "You can see why the Mormons called the Bluff area 'The Hole in the Rock,'" and the tech saying: "If there was a market for rock, we'd all be rich."

Then they dropped into the Gothic Creek Canyon, flying slowly north, with the rimrock of Casa Del Eco Mesa above them and the great eroded hump of the Nokaito Bench to their left. The pilot's voice told Chee they were about two miles upcanyon from the point their sensor map had shown the streaks of migrated radiation along the canyon bottom.

"Be just a few minutes," McKissack said. "Let me know if you see anything interesting."

Chee was leaning his head against the Plexiglas window, seeing the stone cliffs slip slowly past. Here runoff erosion had sliced the sandstone. Here a rockslide had formed a semi-dam below. Here some variation of geology had caused a broad irregular bench to form. In places, the wall was almost sheer pink sandstone. In others, it was layered, marked with dark stripes of coal, the blue of shale, the red where iron ore had colored the rock.

"It ought to be close," McKissack said. "I think we can presume the radiation from the old tailings were washing downstream."

Gothic Creek Canyon had widened a little, and the copter was moving down it slowly and almost eye level with the rimrock to Chee's right. Chee could see another bench sloping up from the canyon floor, supporting a ragtag assortment of chamisa, snakeweed and drought-stunted saltbush. It angled upward toward the broad blackish streak of a coal seam. Then just a few yards ahead and just below Chee saw what he was hoping to see.

"There's a fair-size hole in that coal deposit up ahead," McKissack said. "You think that could be what you're looking for?"

"Could be," Chee said. They slid past the hole, with Chee taking pictures.

"Did you notice that structure above? Up on the mesa?" McKissack asked.

"Could you go up a little so I can get a picture of it?"

The copter rose. Almost directly above the mouth of the mine was the mostly roofless remains of a stone structure. Some of its walls had fallen, and a pyramid-shaped skeleton of pine timbers rose from its center.

"Well now," said McKissack, "does that do it for you?"

"I'm finished, and I thank you," Chee said.

"Unfortunately you're not quite finished," McKissack said. "We have to drag this all the way down to the San Juan, and then back, and then we go back over the mesa and finish our mapping there."

"About how long?"

"About one hour and thirty-four minutes of flying four miles north, making a sharp climbing turn, and flying four miles south, and making a sharp climbing turn and flying four miles north. Doing that until we have the quadrant covered. Then we land, get the tanks rejuiced and do it all over again. Except this time it will be quitting time and we'll knock off for the day."

The next voice was the technician's. "And then

we come back tomorrow and do it all over again with another four-mile-by-four-mile quadrant. Only time the monotony gets broken is when somebody shoots at us."

TWENTY-TWO

JOE LEAPHORN CLEARED away his breakfast dishes, poured himself his second cup of coffee and spread his map on the kitchen table. He was studying it when he heard tires rolling onto the gravel in the parking space in front of his house. He pulled back the curtain and looked out at a dark green and dusty Dodge Ram pickup. The truck was strange to him, but the man who climbed out of it and was hurrying up his walk was Roy Gershwin. Gershwin's expression bespoke trouble.

Leaphorn opened the door, ushered him into the kitchen and said, "What brings you down to Window Rock so early this morning?"

"I got a telephone call last night," Gershwin said. "A threatening call. A man. Sounded like a fairly young man. He said they were going to come after me."

"Who? And come after you for what?"

Gershwin had slumped down in the kitchen chair with his long legs stretched under the table. He looked nervous and angry. "I don't know who," he said. "Well, maybe I could guess. His voice sounded familiar, but I think he had something over his mouth. Or he was trying to talk funny. If it was who I think it was, he's one of those damn militia people. Anyway, it was militia business. The fella said they'd heard I'd been snitching on 'em, and I was going to have to pay for that."

"Well, now," Leaphorn said, "it sounds like you were right to be worrying about those people. Let me get you a cup of coffee."

"I don't want any coffee," Gershwin said. "I want to know what you did to get me screwed like this."

"What I did?" Leaphorn diverted the coffeepot from the fresh cup and refilled his own. "Well, let's see. First, I just thought about what you were asking me to do for you. I couldn't think of any way to do it without getting into a crack—having a choice of either telling a judge you were my source or going to jail for contempt of a court order."

He sat across the table from Gershwin and sipped his coffee. "You sure you don't want a cup?"

Gershwin shook his head.

"So then I went up and talked to people around Bluff and around there about those men. I learned a little about all of them, but more about Jorie," Leaphorn said, watching Gershwin over the rim of his cup. "I decided I'd see if any of them were home. Jorie was."

"Killed himself. That right? So you're the one who found his body."

Leaphorn nodded.

"Paper said he left a suicide note. Is that right?"

"Yeah," Leaphorn said. "There it was." He wondered how he would answer when Gershwin asked him what was in it. But Gershwin didn't ask.

"I wonder why—" Gershwin began, but he cut off the sentence and started again. "The newspaper story sort of said the note was a confession. That he gave the names of the other two. That right?"

Leaphorn nodded.

"Then I don't see why those militia bastards are putting the blame on me." The tone of that was angry, and so was his stare.

"That's a puzzle," Leaphorn said. "Do you think they suspect you know a lot about the robbery plan and were giving that away? Any chance of that?"

"I don't see how that could be. When I was

going to meetings, there was always somebody talking about doing something wild. Something to call attention to their little revolution. But nobody ever talked about robbery."

Leaphorn let it drop. He took another sip of coffee, looked at Gershwin, waited.

Gershwin slammed his fist on the table. "Damn it to hell," he said. "Why can't the cops catch those bastards? They're out there somewhere. They got their names. Know what they look like. Know where they live. Know their habits. It's just like that '98 mess. You got FBI agents swarming around everywhere. You Navajo cops, and the Border Patrol, and four kinds of state cops, and county sheriffs, and twenty other kinds of cops standing around and manning roadblocks. Why in hell can't they get the job done?"

"I don't know," Leaphorn said. "But there's enough canyons out there to swallow up ten thousand cops."

"I guess so. I guess I'm being unreasonable." He shook his head. "To be absolutely honest about it, I'm scared. I'll admit it. That guy that came to the filling station at Bluff the other morning, he could just as easy have come to my house. I could be dead right now. Dead in my bed. Just waiting for somebody to come wandering by and find my body."

Leaphorn tried to think of something reassuring to say. The best he could come up with was that he guessed the bandits would rather run than fight. It didn't seem to console Gershwin.

"You got any idea if the cops are closing in on them? Have they figured out where they might be?"

Leaphorn shook his head.

"If I knew that, I could sleep a little better. Now I can't sleep at all. I just sit in my chair with the lights off and my rifle on my lap." He gave Leaphorn a pleading look. "I'll bet you know something. Long as you was a cop, knowing all the other cops the way you do, and the FBI, they must tell you something."

"The last I heard is pretty much just common knowledge. That stolen truck was abandoned out there on the mesa south of the San Juan, and that's where I understand they're trying to pick up some tracks. South of Bluff and Montezuma Creek and over in the Aneth Oil—"

The buzz of his telephone interrupted him.

He picked it up off the table, said, "Leaphorn."

"This is Jim Chee. We found that mine." Chee's voice was loud with exuberance.

"Oh. Where?"

"You got your map there?"

"Just a minute." Leaphorn slid the map closer, picked up his pen. "OK."

"The mouth is not more than thirty feet below

the canyon rim. About a hundred, hundred and ten feet up from the canyon bottom on a fairly wide shelf. And above it, there's the remains of what must have been a fairly large building. Most of the roof gone now, but a lot of the stone walls still standing. And the framework of what might have been some sort of a hoist sticking up."

"Sounds like what you were hoping to find," Leaphorn said.

"And the reason it fits the theory is you couldn't see the mouth of the mine from the bottom. It's maybe seventy feet up, and hidden by the shelf."

"How'd you find it?"

Chee laughed. "The easy way. Hitched a ride in the EPA helicopter."

Leaphorn still had the pen poised. "Where is it from the place they abandoned the truck?"

"About two miles north—maybe a little less than that."

Leaphorn marked one of his small, precise X's at the proper spot. He glanced at Gershwin.

"What's all this about?" Gershwin asked.

Leaphorn made one of those "just a second" gestures. "Have you notified the FBI?"

"I'm going to call Captain Largo right now," Chee said. "Let him explain it to the federals."

"That sounded interesting," Gershwin said. "Did they find something useful?"

Leaphorn hesitated. "Maybe. Maybe not. They've

been looking for an old, long-abandoned mine out there. One of a thousand places people might hide."

"An old coal mine," Gershwin said. "There's lots of those around. You think it's something I could count on? Sleep easy again?"

Leaphorn shrugged. "You mean, would I bet my life on it?"

"Yeah," Gershwin said. "I guess that's what I mean." He stood, picked up his hat, looked down at the map. "Well, to hell with it. I think I owe you an apology, Joe, storming in here like I did. I'm just going to head on home, pack up my stuff and move out to a motel until this business is over with."

TWENTY-THREE

SERGEANT JIM CHEE limped into Largo's cluttered office feeling even more uneasy than he usually did when approaching the captain. And rightfully so. When he'd pulled into the Navajo Tribal Police parking lot he'd noticed two of the shiny black Ford Taurus FBI sedans. Chee's law-enforcement relationship with the world's largest police force had often been beset with friction. And Captain Largo's telephone call summoning him to this meeting had been even more terse than usual.

"Chee," Largo had said, "get your ass up here."

Now Chee nodded to Special Agent Cabot and the other well-dressed fellow sitting across the desk from the captain and took the chair to which Largo motioned him. He put his cane across his lap and waited.

"You already know Agent Cabot," Largo said. "And this gentleman is Special Agent Smythe." Mutual mumbles and nods followed.

"I've been trying to explain to them why you think this old mine you've found might be the place to look for Ironhand and Baker," Largo said. "They tell me they've already checked every mine deeper than a dog hole up on that mesa. If you've found one they missed, they want to know where it is."

Chee told them, estimating as closely as he could the distance of the mine's canyon mouth from the San Juan and the distance of the surface structure in from the canyon rim.

"You spotted this from a helicopter?" Cabot asked. "Is that correct?"

"That's correct," Chee said.

"Did you know we have prohibited private aircraft flights in that area?" Cabot said.

"I presumed you had," Chee said. "That was a good idea. Otherwise, you'll have those bounty hunters your reward offer is bringing in tying up the air lanes."

This caused a very brief pause while Cabot decided how to respond to this—a not very oblique reminder of the gales of laughter the Bureau had produced in its 1998 fiasco by offering a $250,000 reward one day, and promptly following that with an exhortation for swarms of bounty hunters the offer had attracted to please go away. They hadn't.

Cabot decided to ignore the remark.

"I'll need the name of the company that was operating this aircraft."

"No company, actually," Chee said. "This was a federal-government helicopter."

Cabot looked surprised.

"What agency?"

"It was a Department of Energy copter," Chee said. "I believe it's based at the Tonapaw Proving Grounds over in Nevada."

"Department of Energy? What business do the energy folks have out here?"

Chee had decided he didn't much like Special Agent Cabot, or his attitude, or his well-shined shoes and necktie, or perhaps the fact that Cabot's paycheck was at least twice as large as his, plus all those government perks. He said, "I don't know."

Captain Largo glowered at him.

"I understand the Department of Energy had leased the copter to the EPA," Chee said, and waited for the next question.

"Ah, let's see," said Cabot. "I will rephrase the question so you can understand it. What are the Environmental Protection people doing up here?"

"They're hunting old mines that might be a

threat to the environment," Chee said. "Mapping them. Didn't the Bureau know about that?"

Cabot, used to asking questions and not to answering them, looked surprised again. He hesitated. Glanced at Captain Largo. Chee glanced at Largo, too. Largo's almost-suppressed grin showed that he also knew what Chee was doing and wasn't as upset by it as it had seemed a moment ago.

"I'm sure we did," Cabot said, slightly flushed. "I'm sure if such mapping was in any way helpful to us in this case, it would be used."

Chee nodded. The ball was in the FBI court. He outwaited Cabot, who glanced at Largo again. Largo had found something interesting to look at out the window.

"Sergeant Chee," Cabot said, "Captain Largo told us you had some reason to suspect this particular mine might be used by the perpetrators of the Ute Casino robbery. Would you explain that, please?"

This was the moment Chee had dreaded. He could imagine the amused look on Cabot's face as he tried to explain that the idea came from a Ute tribal legend, trying to describe a hero figure who could jump from canyon bottoms to mesa rims. He took a deep breath and started.

Chee hurried through the relationship of George Ironhand with the original Ironhand, the account of how the Navajos couldn't catch the villain, the notion that since the man was called the Ute name for the badger he might have—like that animal—a hole to hide in with an exit as well as an entrance. As Chee had expected, both Cabot and his partner seemed amused by it. Captain Largo did not appear amused. No suppressed grin now. His expression was dour. Chee found himself talking faster and faster.

"So here was the EPA doing its survey, I hitchhiked a ride, and there it was. The old entrance on a shelf high up on the canyon wall and above it the ruins of the old surface mine. It made sense," Chee said. "I recommended to Captain Largo that it be checked out."

Cabot was studying him. "Let's see now," he said. "You think that the people digging coal out of the cliff down in the canyon decided to dig right on up to the top? If I know my geology at all, that would have them digging through several thick levels of sandstone and all sorts of other strata. Isn't that right?"

"Actually, I was thinking more of digging down from the top," Chee said.

"Can you describe the old mine structure?" Cabot asked. "The building?"

"I have pictures of it," Chee said. "I took my Polaroid camera along." He handed Cabot two photos of the old structures, one shot from rim level and one from a higher angle.

Cabot looked at them, then handed them to his partner.

"Is that the one you thought it might be?" he asked.

"That's it," Smythe said. "We spotted that the day we found their truck. We put a crew in there that afternoon and searched it, along with all the other buildings on that mesa."

"What did you find?" asked Cabot, who obviously already knew the answer. "Did you see any sign that people might be hiding in the mine shaft?"

Smythe looked amused. "We didn't even see a shaft," he said. "Much less people. Just lots of rodent droppings, old, old trash, odds and ends of broken equipment, animal tracks, three empty Thunderbird wine bottles with well-aged labels. There was no sign at all of human occupancy. Not in recent years."

Cabot handed Chee the photographs, smiling. "You might want these for your scrapbook," he said.

TWENTY-FOUR

As was his lifelong habit, Joe Leaphorn had gone to bed early.

Professor Louisa Bourebonette had returned from her Ute-myth-collecting expedition late. The sound of the car door shutting outside his open window had awakened him. He lay listening to her talking to Conrad Becenti about some esoteric translation problem. He heard her coming in, doing something in the kitchen, opening and closing the door to what had been Emma's private working space and their guest bedroom, then silence. He analyzed his feelings about all this: having another person in the house, having another woman using Emma's space and assorted related issues. He reached no conclusions. The next thing he knew the sunlight was on his face, he heard his Mister Coffee making those strangling sounds signaling its work was done, and it was morning.

Louisa was scrambling eggs at the stove.

"I know you like 'em scrambled," she said, "because that's the way you always order them."

"True," Leaphorn said, thinking that sometimes he liked them scrambled, and sometimes fried, and rarely poached. He poured both of them a cup of coffee, and sat.

"I had a fairly productive day," she said, serving the eggs. "The old fellow in the nursing home at Cortez told us a version of the Ute migration story I've never heard before. How about you?"

"Gershwin came to see me."

"Really? What did he want?"

"To tell the truth, I've been wondering about that. I don't really know."

"So what did he say he wanted? I'll bet he didn't come just to thank you."

Leaphorn chuckled. "He said he'd had a threatening telephone call. Someone accusing him of tipping off the police. He said he was scared, and he seemed to be. He wanted to know what was being done to catch them. If the police had any idea where they were. He said he was going to move into a motel somewhere until this was over."

"Might be a big motel bill," Louisa said. "Those

two guys from the 1998 jobs are still out there, I guess. I hear the FBI has quit suggesting they're dead."

"Yeah," Leaphorn said. He drank coffee, buttered his toast, ate eggs that were scrambled just a bit too dry for his taste and tried to decide what it was about Gershwin's visit that was bothering him.

"Something's on your mind," Louisa said. "Is it the crime?"

"I guess. It's none of my business anymore, but some things puzzle me."

Louisa had consumed only toast and was cleaning up around the stove.

"I'm heading south to Flagstaff," she said. "I'll go through all these notes. I'll take this wonderful old myth that has been floating around free as the air all these generations and punch it into my computer. Then one of these days I will call it up out of the hard disk and petrify it in a paper for whichever scholarly publication will want it."

"You don't sound very eager," Leaphorn said. "Why not let that wait another day and come along with me?"

Louisa had made her speech facing the sink, where she was rinsing his frying pan. Pan in hand, she turned.

"Where? Doing what?"

Leaphorn thought about that. A good question. How to explain?

"Actually doing what I do sometimes when I can't figure something out. I drive off somewhere, and walk around for a while, or just sit on a rock and hope for inspiration. Sometimes I get it, sometimes not."

Professor Bourebonette's expression said she liked the sound of that.

"Being a social scientist, I think I'd like to observe that operation," she said.

And so they left the professor's car behind and headed south in Leaphorn's pickup, taking Navajo Route 12 north, with the sandstone cliffs of the Manuelito Plateau off to their right, the great emptiness of Black Creek Valley on the left, and clouds lit by the morning sun building over the Painted Cliffs ahead of them.

"You said some things were bothering you," Louisa said. "Like what?"

"I called an old friend of mine up at Cortez. Marci Trujillo. She used to be with a bank up there that did business with the Ute Casino. I told her I thought that four-hundred-and-something-thousand-dollar estimate of the loot sounded a little high to me. She said it sounded just about right for an end-of-the-month payday Friday night."

"Wow," Louisa said. "And that mostly comes from people who can't afford to lose it. I think you Navajos were smart to say no to gambling."

"I guess so," Leaphorn said.

"On the other hand, in the old days when the Utes were stealing your horses they had to come down and get 'em. Now you drive up there and hand over the cash."

Leaphorn nodded. "So I told her I was guessing that the loot would be mostly in smaller bills. A very few hundreds or fifties, and mostly twenties, tens, fives, and ones. She said that was a good guess. So I asked her how much that would weigh."

"Weigh?"

"She said if we decide the median of bills in the loot was about ten dollars, which she thought would be close, that would be forty-five thousand bills. The weight of that would be just about one hundred and seven pounds and eleven ounces."

"I can't believe this," Louisa said. "Right off the top of her head?"

"No. She had to do some arithmetic. She said banks get their money supply in counted bundles. They put the bundles on special scales to make sure someone with sticky fingers isn't slipping a bill out here and there."

Louisa shook her head. "There's so much going on out in the real world we academics don't know about." She paused, thinking. "For example, now I'm wondering how any of this is causing you to get suspicious about Gershwin's visit."

"Ms. Trujillo once ran the bank Everett Jorie used. I asked her if she could tell me anything about Jorie's financial situation. She said probably not, but since Jorie was dead and his account frozen until an estate executor showed up, she could maybe give me some general hints. She said Jorie had both a checking and a savings account. He had 'some' balance in the first one and 'several thousand dollars' in the other. Plus a fine credit rating."

"Then why in the world—But he said it was to help finance their little revolution, didn't he? I guess that explains it. But it doesn't explain how you knew where Jorie did his banking."

"The checkbook was on Jorie's desk," Leaphorn said.

Louisa was grinning at him. "Oh, really," she said. "Right out there in plain sight just where people keep their checkbooks. Wasn't that convenient for you?"

Leaphorn chuckled. "Well, maybe I had to inch open a desk drawer a little. But anyway, then I asked if Ray Gershwin banked with her, and she said not now, but he used to. They'd turned him down for a loan last spring, and Gershwin had gotten sore about it and moved his business elsewhere. And did she know anything about Gershwin's current solvency. She laughed and said it was bad last spring, and she doubted if it was going to get any better. I asked why not, and she said Gershwin may lose his biggest grazing lease. Some sort of litigation is pending in federal court. So I called the district court clerk up in Denver to ask about that. He called me back and said the case was moot. The plaintiff had died."

Silence. Leaphorn angled to the right off of Navajo Route 12 onto New Mexico Highway 134.

"Now we cross Washington Pass," he said. "Named after the governor of New Mexico Territory who thought this part of the world was full of gold, silver and so forth and was an early believer in ethnic cleansing. He's the one who sent Kit Carson and the New Mexico Hispanos and the Utes to round us up and get rid of us—once and for all. The Tribal Council got the government to agree to change the name a few years ago, but everybody still calls it Washington Pass. I guess that proves we Navajos don't hold grudges. We're tolerant."

"I'm not," Louisa said. "I'm tired of waiting for you to tell me the name of the deceased plaintiff."

"I'll bet you've already guessed."

"Everett Jorie?"

"Right. Interesting, isn't it?"

"Yes. Let me think about it."

She did. "That could be a motive for murder, couldn't it?"

"Good enough I'd think."

"And lots of irony there," Louisa said, "if irony is the word for it. It reminds you of one of those awful wildlife films you're always seeing on television. The lions pull down the zebra, and then the jackals and the buzzards move in to take advantage. Only this time it's old Mr. Timms, trying to defraud his insurance company, and Mr. Gershwin, trying to get rid of a lawsuit."

"Doesn't do a lot for one's opinion of humanity," Leaphorn said.

Louisa was still looking thoughtful. "I'll bet you know this district court clerk personally, don't you? If I called the federal district court and asked for the court clerk, I'd get shifted around four or five times, put on hold, and finally get somebody who'd tell me he couldn't release that information, or I had to drive up to Denver and get it from the judge or something like that." Louisa was sounding slightly resentful. "This all-encompassing, eternal, universal, everlasting good-old-boy network. You do know him, don't you?"

"I confess," Leaphorn said. "But you know, it's a small world up here in this empty country. Work as a cop as long as I did, you know about everybody who has anything to do with the law."

"I guess so," Louisa said. "So he said he'd trot down and look it up for you?"

"I think it's just punch the proper keys on his computer and up comes Jorie, Everett, Plaintiff, and a list of petitions filed under that name. Something like that. He said this Jorie did a lot of business with the federal court. And he was also suing our Mr. Timms. Some sort of a claim he was violating rights of neighboring leaseholders by unauthorized use of BLM land for an airport."

"Well, now. That's nice. A Department of Defense spokesman would call that peripheral damage."

"Peripheral benefit in this case," Leaphorn said.

"It's collateral damage. But how about the suicide note?"

"Remember it wasn't handwritten on paper," Leaphorn said. "It was typed into a computer. Anyone could have done it. And remember that last manhunt. One of the perps turned up dead and the FBI declared him a suicide. That might have given somebody the idea that the feds would go for that notion again."

Louisa laughed. "You know what I'm wondering? Did the neat little trick Mr. Timms tried to pull off suggest to retired lieutenant Joe Leaphorn that Gershwin might have seen the same opportunity to deal with a lawsuit?"

Leaphorn grinned. "As a matter of fact, I think it did."

Near the crest of Washington Pass he pulled off the pavement onto a dirt track that led through a grove of Ponderosa pines. He pulled to a stop at the edge of a cliff and gestured northwest. Below them lay a vast landscape dappled with cloud shadows and late-morning sunlight and rimmed north and east by the shapes of mesas and mountains. They stood on the rimrock, just looking.

"Wow," Louisa said. "I never get enough of this."

"It's home country for me," Leaphorn said. "Emma used to get me to drive up here and look at it those times I was thinking of taking a job in Washington." He pointed northeast. "We lived right down there when I was a boy, about ten miles down between the Two Grey Hills Trading Post and Toadlena. My mother planted my umbilical cord under a piñon on the hill behind our hogan." He chuckled. "Emma knew the legend. That's the binding the wandering child can never break."

"You still miss her, don't you?"

"I will always miss her," Leaphorn said.

Louisa put her arm around him and hugged.

"Southeast," she said. "That hump of clouds. Could that be Mount Taylor?"

"It is, and that's why its other name—I should say one of its other names—is Mother of Rains. The westerlies are pushed up there, and the mist becomes rain in the colder air and then the clouds drift on, dumping the moisture before they get to Albuquerque."

"*Tsoodzil* in Navajo," Louisa said, "and the Turquoise Mountain when you translate it into English, and Dark Mountain for the Rio Grande Pueblos, and your Sacred Mountain of the East."

"And due north, maybe forty miles, there's Shiprock sticking up like a finger pointing at the sky, and, beyond, that blue bump on the horizon is the nose of Sleeping Ute Mountain."

"Scene of the crime," Louisa said.

Leaphorn said nothing. He was frowning, looking north. He drew in a deep breath, let it out.

"What?" Louisa said. "Why this sudden look of worry?"

He shook his head.

"I'm not sure," he said. "Let's drive on down to Two Grey Hills. I want to call Chee. I want to make sure the Bureau sent some people in to check out that old mine."

"I always wonder why you don't have a cell phone. Don't they work well out here?"

"Until I quit being a cop I had a radio in my vehicle," Leaphorn said. "When I quit being a cop, I didn't have anybody to call."

Which sounded sort of sad to Louisa. "What's this about a mine?" she asked, as they got back into the vehicle.

"Maybe I didn't mention that," Leaphorn said.

"Chee was looking for an old Mormon coal mine, abandoned in the nineteenth century that maybe had a canyon entrance and another one from the top of the mesa. Where they could lift the coal out without climbing out of the canyon carrying it. I thought that might have been the hideout of Ironhand's dad. It would explain that business Old Lady Bashe was telling you about him disappearing in the canyon and reappearing on top."

"Yes," Louisa said. "You're thinking that's where those two are hiding now?"

"Yeah," Leaphorn said. "Just a possibility." He turned the truck left, down the bumpy dirt road and away from the highway. "This is rough going," he said. "But if you don't break something, its only about nine miles this way. If you go around by the highway, it's almost thirty."

"Which tells me you're in a hurry to make this telephone call. You want to tell me why?"

"I want to make sure he told the FBI," Leaphorn said, and laughed. "He's awful touchy about the Bureau. Gets his feelings hurt. And if he did tell them, I want to find out if they followed up on it."

Louisa waited, glanced at him, braced herself as the truck crossed a rocky washout and tilted down the slope.

"That doesn't tell me why you're worried. All of a sudden."

TONY HILLERMAN

"Because I'm remembering how interested Gershwin was in the location of that mine."

She thought about that. "It seems reasonable. If somebody threatens you, you're going to wonder where they're hanging out."

"Right," Leaphorn said. "Probably nothing to worry about."

But he didn't slow down.

TWENTY-FIVE

SERGEANT JIM CHEE was in his house-trailer home, sprawled in his chair with his foot perched on a pillow on his bunk and a Ziploc bag full of crushed ice draped over his ankle. Bernadette Manuelito was at the stove preparing a pot of coffee and being very quiet about it because Chee wasn't in the mood for conversation or anything else.

He had gone over everything that had happened in Largo's office, suffered again the humiliation of Cabot handing him his photos of the mine, Cabot's snide smile, being more or less dismissed by Captain Largo, slinking out of the room without a shred of dignity left. And then, his head full of outrage, indignation and self-disgust, not paying attention to where the hell he was walking, losing his balance tripping over something in the parking lot, and coming down full weight on his sprained ankle and dumping himself full length on the gravel.

And of course a swarm of the various sorts of cops working on the casino hunt had been there to see this—two of his NTP officers reporting in, the division radio gal coming out, three or four Border Patrol trackers up from El Paso, a BIA cop he'd once worked with, and a couple of the immense oversupply of FBI agents standing around picking their noses and waiting for Cabot to emerge. And of course, when he was pushing himself up—awkwardly trying to keep any pressure off the ankle—there was Bernie taking his arm.

And now here was Bernie in his trailer, puttering with his coffeepot. Largo had emerged and, despite Chee's objections, had dispatched Bernie to take him to the clinic to have the ankle looked after. She had done that, and brought him home, and now it was past quitting time for her shift but here she was anyway, measuring the coffee on her own time.

And looking pretty as she did it. He resisted thinking about that, unwilling to diminish the self-pity he was enjoying. But looking at her, as neat from the rear elevation as from the front, reminded him that he was comparing her with Janet Pete. She lacked Janet's high-gloss glamour, her physical perfection (depending, however, on how one rated that) and her sophistication. Again, how did one rate sophistication? Did you rate it by the standards of the Ivy League, Stanford and the rest of the politically correct privileged class, or by the Chuska Mountain sheep-camp society, where sophistication required the deeper and more difficult knowledge of how one walked in beauty, content in a difficult world? Such thoughts were causing Chee to feel better, and he turned his mind hurriedly back to the memory of Cabot returning his photographs, thereby restoking his anger.

Just then the telephone rang. It was the Legendary Lieutenant himself—the very one whose notions about Ute tribal legends was at the root of this humiliation.

"Did you report finding that mine to the Bureau?"

"Yes," Chee said.

Silence. Leaphorn had expected more than that.

"What's being done about it? Do you know?"

"Nothing."

"Nothing?" Leaphorn's tone said he couldn't believe that.

"That's right," Chee said. He realized he was playing the same childish game with Leaphorn that he had played with Cabot. He didn't like the feel of that. He admired Leaphorn. Leaphorn, he had to admit it, was his friend. So he interrupted the silence.

"The Special Agent involved said they'd already searched that mine. Nothing in it but animal tracks and mice droppings. He handed me back the photos I'd taken, and they sent me on my way."

"Be damned," Leaphorn said. Chee could hear him breathing for a while. "Did he say when they did their search?"

"He said right after the truck was found. He said they searched the whole area. Everything."

"Yeah," Leaphorn said. "How much structure was left on top of the mesa?"

"Some stone walls, partly fallen down, roof gone from part of it. Then there was a framework of timbers, sort of a triangle structure, sticking out of it."

"Sounds like the support for the tipple to lift the coal out and dump it."

"I guess so," Chee said, wondering about the point of all this. The feds had looked, and nobody was home.

"Searched the whole area, you said? That day?"

"Yeah," Chee said, sensing Leaphorn's point and feeling a faint stir of illogical optimism.

"Didn't Deputy Dashee say they found the truck about middle of the day?"

"Yeah," Chee said. "And they'd be searching

the Timms place, house, barns, outbuildings, and all those roads wandering around to those Mobil Oil pump stations, and—" Chee ran out of other examples. Casa Del Eco Mesa was huge, but it was almost mostly empty hugeness.

"The best they would have had time to do would be to give it a quick glance," Leaphorn said.

"Well, yes. Wouldn't that be enough to show it was empty?"

"I think I'll take a drive up there and look around for myself. Is that area still roadblocked?"

"It was yesterday," Chee said. Then he added exactly what he knew the Legendary Lieutenant hoped he would add. "I'll go with you and show 'em my badge."

"Fine," Leaphorn said. "I'm calling from Two Grey Hills. Professor Bourebonette is with me, but she's run into a couple of her fellow professors dickering over a rug. Hold on. Let me find out if they can give her a ride back to Flagstaff."

Chee waited.

"Yep," Leaphorn said. "I'll pick you up soon as I can get there."

"Right. I'll be ready."

Bernadette Manuelito was staring at him. "Wait a minute," she said. "Go where with whom? You can't go anywhere with that ankle. You're supposed to keep it elevated. And iced."

Chee relaxed, closed his eyes, recognized that

he was feeling much, much better. Why did talking to Joe Leaphorn do that for him? And now this business with Bernie. Worrying about his ankle. Bossing him around. Why did that make him feel so much better? He opened his eyes and looked up at her. A very pretty young lady even when she was frowning at him.

TWENTY-SIX

SERGEANT JIM CHEE kept his ankle elevated by resting it on pillows on the rear seat of Officer Bernie Manuelito's battered old Unit 11. He kept it iced with a plastic sack loaded with ice cubes. The ankle was feeling better, and so was Chee. Going to the clinic and having it expertly wrapped and taped had done wonders for the injury. Having his old boss showing him some respect had been good for bruised morale.

Bernie was tooling westward on U.S. 160, past the Red Mesa School, heading toward the Navajo 35 intersection at Mexican Water. Chee was behind her, slumped against the driver's side of the car, watching the side of Leaphorn's graying burr haircut. The lieutenant was not nearly as taciturn as Chee remembered him. He was telling her of the names Gershwin had left on the note at the Navajo Inn coffee shop, and how that had led to Jorie's place and about learning Jorie was suing Gershwin and the rest of it. Bernie was hanging on every word, and Leaphorn was obviously enjoying the attention. He'd been explaining to her why he had always been skeptical of coincidence, and Chee had heard that so often when he was the man's assistant in the Window Rock office that he had it memorized. It was bedrock Navajo philosophy. All things interconnected. No effect without cause. The beetle's wing affects the breeze, the lark's song bends the warrior's mood, a cloud back on the western horizon parts, lets light of the setting sun through, turns the mountains to gold, affects the mood and decision of the Navajo Tribal Council. Or, as the Anglo poet had put it, "No man is an island."

And Bernie, in her kindly fashion, was recognizing a lonely man's need and asking all the right questions. What a girl. "Is that sort of how you use that map Sergeant Chee tells me about?" And of course it was.

"I think Jim's mind works about the way mine does," Leaphorn said. "And I hope he'll correct me if I'm wrong. This casino business, for example. The casino's by Sleeping Ute Mountain. The escape vehicle is abandoned a hundred miles west on Casa Del Eco Mesa. Nearby a barn with an aircraft in it. The same day the aircraft is stolen. Closeness in both time and place. Nearby is an old mine. The Ute legends suggest the father of one of the bandits used it as his escape route. A little cluster of coincidences."

Bernie said, "Yes," but she sounded doubtful.

"There are more," Leaphorn said. "Remember the Great 1998 Manhunt. Three men involved. Police shot, stolen vehicle abandoned. Huge hunt begins. The fellow believed to be the ringleader is found dead. The FBI rules it suicide. The other two men vanish in the canyons."

Now that his ankle was no longer painful, Chee was feeling drowsy. He let his head slide over against the upholstery. Yawned. How long had it been since he'd had a good sleep?

"Another coincidence," Bernie agreed. "You have your doubts about that one, too?"

"Jim suggested the first crime might have been the cause of the second one," Leaphorn said.

Chee was no longer sleepy. What did that mean? He couldn't remember saying that.

"Ah," Bernie said. "That's going to take some complicated thinking. And that could go for the other ones, too. For example, seeing the abandoned truck and hearing about the robbery on the radio, Mr. Timms saw a way to get rid of his airplane. He claimed it was stolen and filed an insurance claim."

"It would be cause and effect that way, too, of

course," Leaphorn said. "Or perhaps the airplane was the reason the car was abandoned where it was, as the FBI originally concluded."

Chee sat up. *What the devil is Leaphorn driving at?*

"I'm afraid I'm lost," Bernie said.

"Let me give you a whole new theory of the crime," Leaphorn said. "Let's say it went like this. Someone up in this border country paid close attention to the 1998 crime, and it suggested to him the way to solve a problem. Actually two problems. It would supply him with some needed cash, and it would eliminate an enemy. Let's say this person has connections with the militia, or the survivalists, or EarthFirsters, or any of the radical groups. Let's say he recruits two or three men to help him, pretending they're going after the money to finance their political cause. He gets Mr. Timms involved. Either he leases the airplane in advance for a flight or he lets Timms in on the crime. Offers him a slice of the loot."

"You're talking about Everett Jorie," Bernie said.

"I could be, yes," Leaphorn said. "But in my proposal, Jorie has the role of the enemy to be eliminated."

Chee cleared his throat. "Wait a minute, Lieutenant," he said. "How about the suicide note? All that?"

Leaphorn looked around at Chee, gave him a

wry look. "I had the advantage of being there. Seeing the man where he lived. Seeing what he read. His library. The sort of stuff he treasured, that made up his life. When I look back at it, it makes me think I'm showing my age. If you or Officer Manuelito had been the ones to find the body, to see it all, you would have gotten suspicious a long time before I did."

Chee was thinking he still didn't feel suspicious. But he said, "OK. How did it work?"

Bernie had slowed. "Is that where you want me to turn? That dirt road?"

"It's rough, but it's a lot shorter than driving down to 191 and then having to cut back."

"I'm in favor of short," Bernie said, and they were bumping off the pavement and onto the dirt.

"I'd guess this is the route the casino perps took," Leaphorn said. "They must have known this mesa, living out here, and they must have known it led them into a dead-end situation." He laughed. "Another argument for my unorthodox theory of the crime. Having them turn off 191 and get lost would be too much of a coincidence for my taste."

"Lieutenant," Chee said, "why don't you go ahead and tell us what happened at Jorie's place."

"What I think may have happened," Leaphorn said. "Well, let's say that our villain knocks on

Jorie's door, points the fatal pistol at Jorie, marches him into Jorie's office, has Jorie sit in his computer chair, then shoots him point-blank so it will pass as a suicide. Then he turns on the computer, leans over the body, types out the suicide note, leaves the computer on, and departs the scene."

"Why?" Chee asked. "Actually about four or five whys. I think I can see some of the motives, but some of it's hazy."

"Jorie was one of these fellows who thrive on litigation. And being a lawyer and admitted to the Utah bar, he could file all the suits he liked without it costing him much. He had two suits pending against our man. He was even suing Timms. Claimed his little airplane panicked his cattle, causing weight loss, loss of calves, so forth. Another suit claimed Timms violated his grazing lease with that unauthorized landing strip. But Timms isn't my choice of villains. Another one of Jorie's suits was aimed at canceling our villain's Bureau of Land Management lease."

"We're talking about Mr. Gershwin, of course," Chee said. "Aren't we?"

"In theory, yes," Leaphorn said.

"All right," Chee said. "What's next?"

"Now he has eliminated one of his two problems—the enemy and his troublesome lawsuits. But not the other one."

"The money," Bernie said. "You mean he'd only get a third of that?"

"In my theory, I think it's a little more complicated," Leaphorn replied. He looked back at Chee. "You remember in that suicide note, how he told the FBI where to find his two partners, how he stressed that they had sworn never to be taken alive. If they were caught, they wanted to go into history for the number of cops they had killed."

"His plan to eliminate them," Chee said, and produced a wry laugh. "It probably would have worked. If those guys were militia members, they'd have their heads full of how the FBI behaved at Ruby Ridge and Waco. Frankly, if I was going in with the SWAT team, I think I'd be blazing away."

"There must have seemed to be a flaw in that plan, though. Our villain had to wonder how the suicide note would be found. No one had any reason to suspect Jorie. Not a clue to any of the identities. So our villain solved that by finding himself a not-very-bright retired cop who he could trust to tip off the FBI without getting him involved in it."

"I'll be damned," Chee said. "I wondered how you happened to be the one who found Jorie's body."

"What was the rush?" Bernie asked. "Sooner or later Jorie would have been missed. Somebody would have gone out to see about him. You know how people out here are."

"My theoretical villain didn't think he could wait for that. He didn't want to risk the cops catching his partners before the cops knew about their plan to go down killing cops. Captured alive, they'd know just exactly who'd turned them in. They'd even the score and get off easier by testifying against him."

"Yeah," Bernie said. "That makes sense."

Chee was leaning forward now. He tapped Leaphorn's shoulder. "Look. Lieutenant, I didn't mean that the way it sounded. Like I thought you weren't very bright."

"Matter of fact I wasn't. He got almost exactly what he wanted out of me."

Which was true, but Chee let that hang.

"The only thing that went wrong was his partners must have smelled something in the wind. They didn't go home like they were supposed to— safe in the notion that the police hadn't a clue to who they were. They didn't wait for the SWAT teams to arrive and mow them down. They slipped away and hid somewhere."

"The old Mormon mine," Chee said. "So why didn't the FBI find them there?"

"I don't know," Leaphorn said. "Maybe they were somewhere else when the federal agents took a look. Maybe they went home, as our vil-

lain probably told them to do, and then got uneasy and came back to Ironhand's dad's hideaway,
to wait and see what happened. Or maybe the
federals didn't look hard enough. They'd have
had no way of knowing about the entrance down
in the canyon."

"That's true," Chee said. "You couldn't see it
from the bottom. And, of course, we don't know
if the bottom mine connects to the top."

Bernie laughed. "I don't know," she said. "I like
to believe in legends. Even if they're Ute legends."

"I've just been along for the ride," Chee said.
"Just giving my ankle an airing. Now I'm wondering what the plan is. I hope it's not that we
walk up to that mine and order Baker and Ironhand to come out with their hands up."

"No," Leaphorn said, and laughed.

"Bernie would have to handle that all by herself," Chee said. "You're a civilian. I'm on sick leave
or something. Let's say I'm back on vacation."

"But you did bring your pistol, I'll bet," Bernie
said. "You did, didn't you?"

"I think I've got it here somewhere. You know
the rules. Don't leave home without it."

"What I'd like to do is drop in on Mr. Timms,"
Leaphorn said. "I think we can get him to cooperate. And if he does, and if I'm guessing right, then
Officer Manuelito gets on her radio and summons
reinforcements."

"Why couldn't we call in for a backup and then—" Chee cut off the rest of that. He imagined Leaphorn explaining his theory to Special Agent Cabot—asking backup to check a mine the FBI had already certified free of fugitives. He imagined Cabot's smirk. He switched to another question.

"Do you know Mr. Timms?" he asked. Another stupid question. Of course he did. Leaphorn knew everyone in the Four Corners. At least everyone over sixty.

"Not well," Leaphorn said. "Haven't seen him for years. But I think we can get him to cooperate."

Chee leaned back against the door and watched the desert landscape slide past. He imagined Timms telling them to go to hell. He imagined Timms ordering them off his property.

But then he relaxed. Retired or not, Leaphorn was still the Legendary Lieutenant.

TWENTY-SEVEN

BERNIE LET UNIT 11 roll to a stop just in front of the Timms front porch, and they sat for the few moments required by empty-country courtesy to give the occupant time to get himself decent and prepare to acknowledge visitors. The door opened. A tall, skinny, slightly stooped man stood in the doorway looking out at them.

Leaphorn got out, Bernie followed, and Chee moved his ankle off the pillow and onto the floor. It hurt, but not much.

"Hello, Mr. Timms," Leaphorn said. "I wonder if you remember me."

Timms stepped out onto the porch, the sunlight reflecting from his spectacles. "Maybe I do," he said. "Didn't you used to be Corporal Joe Leaphorn with the Navajo Police? Wasn't you the one who helped out when that fellow was shooting at my airplane?"

"Yes sir," Leaphorn said. "That was me. And this young lady is Officer Bernadette Manuelito."

"Well, come on in out of the sun," Timms said.

Chee couldn't stand the thought of missing this. He pushed the car door open with his good foot, got his cane and limped across the yard, eyes on the ground to avoid an accident, noticing that the bedroom slipper he was wearing on his left foot was collecting sandburrs. "And this," Leaphorn was saying, "is Sergeant Jim Chee. He and I worked together."

"Yes sir," Timms said, and held out his hand. The shake was Navajo fashion, less grip and more the gentle touch. An old-timer who knew the culture. And so nervous that the muscles in his cheek were twitching.

"Wasn't expecting company, so I don't have anything fixed, but I could offer you something cold to drink," Timms said, ushering them into a small, dark room cluttered with the sort of old mismatched furniture one collects from Goodwill Industries shops.

"I don't think we should accept your hospitality, Mr. Timms," Leaphorn said. "We came here on some serious business."

"On that insurance claim," Timms said. "I

already sent off a letter canceling that. Already did that."

"I'm afraid it's a lot more serious than that," Leaphorn said.

"That's the trouble with getting old. You get so damned forgetful," Timms said, talking fast. "I get up to get me a drink of water and by the time I get to the icebox I forget what I'm in the kitchen for. I flew that old L-17 down there to do some work, and then a fella offered me a ride home and I went off and left it and then we were hearing about the robbery on the radio and when I got home and saw the barn open and my airplane gone I just thought—"

Timms stopped. He stared at Leaphorn. So did Bernie. So did Chee.

"More than that?" Timms asked.

Leaphorn stood silent, eyes on Timms.

"What more?" Timms asked. He slumped down into an overstuffed armchair, looking up at Leaphorn.

"You remember that fellow who was doing the shooting when you flew over his place? Everett Jorie."

"He quit doing that after you talked to him." Timms tried a smile, which didn't come off. "I appreciated that. Now he's turned into a bandit. Robbed that casino. Killed himself."

"It looked like that for a while," Leaphorn said.

Timms shrank into the chair. Raised his right hand to his forehead. He said, "You saying somebody killed him?"

Leaphorn let the question hang for a moment. Said: "How well do you know Roy Gershwin?"

Timms opened his mouth, closed it, and looked up at Leaphorn. Chee found himself feeling sorry for the man. He looked terrified.

"Mr. Timms," Leaphorn said, "you are in a position right now to help yourself a lot. The FBI isn't happy with you. Hiding that airplane, reporting it stolen, that slowed down the hunt for those killers a lot. It's not the sort of thing law enforcement forgets. Unless it has a reason to want to overlook it. If you're helpful, then the police tend to say 'Well, Mr. Timms was just forgetful.' If you're not helpful, then things like that tend to go to the grand jury to let the jury decide whether you were what they call an accessory after the fact. And that's not insurance fraud. That's in a murder case."

"Murder case. You mean Jorie?"

"Mr. Timms," Leaphorn said, "tell me about Roy Gershwin."

"He was by here today," Timms said. "You just missed him."

Now it was Leaphorn's turn to look startled. And Chee's.

"What did he want? What did he say?"

"Not much. He wanted directions to that old Latter-Day-Saints mine. The place those Mormons used to dig their coal. And I told him, and he run right out of here. In a big hurry."

"I think we'd better go," Leaphorn said, and started for the door.

Timms looked sick. He made a move to rise, sank back.

"You telling me Gershwin killed that Everett Jorie? Don't tell me that."

Leaphorn and Bernie were already out the door, and as Chee limped after them he heard Timms saying, "Oh, God. I was afraid of that."

TWENTY-EIGHT

IT WAS EASY enough to notice where Gershwin's pickup had turned off the track, easy to see the path it had left through the crusted blowsand and broken clusters of snakeweed. Following the tracks was a different matter. Gershwin's truck had better traction and much higher clearance than Bernie's Unit 11 patrol car, which, under its official paint, was still a worn-out Chevy sedan.

It lost traction on the side of one of those great humps that wind erosion drifts around Mormon tea in desert climates. It slid sideways, rear wheels down the slope. Leaphorn checked Bernie's instinct to gun the engine by a sharply whispered "No!"

"I think we're about as close as we want to drive," he said. "I'll take a look."

He took the unit's binoculars out of the glove

box, opened the door, slid out, walked up the hummock, stood for a minute looking and then walked back.

"The mine structure is maybe a quarter mile," he said, pointing. "Over by the rimrock. Gershwin's truck is about two hundred yards ahead of us. It looks empty. It also looks like he left it where it couldn't be seen from the mine."

"So now what?" Chee said. "Do we radio in and ask for some backup?" Even as he asked, he was wondering how that call would sound. Imagining the exchange. An area rancher had driven his pickup over to an old mine site. Why do you need backup? Because we think the casino perps are hiding there. Which mine? One the FBI has already checked out and certified as empty.

Leaphorn was looking at him, quizzically.

"Or what?" Chee concluded, thinking that surely Leaphorn wouldn't propose they simply walk up, ask if anybody was inside and tell them to come out and surrender.

"We're on their blind side," Leaphorn said. "Why don't we get closer? See if we can learn what's going on."

"You brought your piece," Leaphorn said. "I'm going to borrow Officer Manuelito's pistol. Officer Manuelito, I want you to stay here close to the radio but get up on the hump there where you can see what's going on. We may need you to make some fast contacts. I'll borrow your side-arm."

"Give you my gun?" Bernie said, sounding doubtful.

Chee was easing himself out of the car, thinking that the Legendary Lieutenant had forgotten he was a civilian. He had unilaterally rescinded his retirement and resumed his rank.

"Your pistol," he said, holding out his hand. Bernie's expression switched from doubtful to determined.

"No, sir. That's one of the first things we learn. We keep our pistols."

Leaphorn stared at her. Nodded. "You're right," he said. "Hand me the rifle."

She pulled it out of the rack and handed it to him, butt first. He checked the chamber.

"In fact, Manuelito, I want you to get into radio contact now. Tell 'em where we are, precisely as you can, tell them that Sergeant Chee is checking an old mine building and we may need some support. Tell them you're going to be out of the car a few minutes to back him up and ask them to stand by. Then I want you on top of that hummock up there watching what's going on. Doing what needs to be done."

"Sergeant Chee should stay here," Bernie said. "He can't walk that far. I'll go with you. He can handle the radio."

Chee used his sergeant voice. "Manuelito, you'll do the radio. That's an order."

Whatever the reason, the excitement, the adrenaline pumping, perhaps the distracting notion that in a few minutes an award-winning Green Beret sniper might be shooting him, Chee limped up the hummock slope hardly aware of his bandaged ankle or the sand in his bedroom slipper. The ruined mine structure came into view, the back side of what he had photographed from the helicopter. As Leaphorn had said, this side presented only a windowless stone wall.

Leaphorn pointed, noted the entrance door was probably to their left, pointed out the route down the gentle slope that Chee should take, noting the cover available in the event anyone came out of the structure. Any pretense of being a civilian, of being anything except the Navajo Tribal Police officer in charge, had ceased to exist.

"I'll move down to the right," Leaphorn concluded. "Watch for a signal. If anyone comes out, we'll let them get far enough from the structure. They, or he, will probably be walking toward Gershwin's truck. We'll see what opportunity presents itself."

"Yes sir," Chee said. He rechecked his pistol and did exactly as told.

About five minutes, and fifty cautious yards later, Chee first heard a voice.

He stood, waved at Leaphorn, pointed to the wall and made talking motions with his hand. Leaphorn nodded.

A moment later, the sound of laughter.

Then the sharp door-slam sound of a pistol shot. Then another, and another.

Chee looked at Leaphorn, who was looking at him. Leaphorn signaled him to stay down. They waited. Time ticked past. Leaphorn signaled him to close in and moved slowly toward the wall. Chee did the same.

A tall, elderly man emerged from behind the wall. What seemed to be a student's backpack dangled from one hand. He was wearing a white shirt with the tail out, jeans and a tan straw hat. As Leaphorn had predicted, he walked toward Gershwin's truck.

Chee ducked back out of sight behind a growth of saltbush, following the man with his pistol. No more than twenty yards. An easy shot if a shooting was called for.

Leaphorn was standing in the open, the rifle cradled across his arm.

"Mr. Gershwin," he shouted. "Roy. What are you doing way out here?"

Gershwin stopped, stood frozen for a moment, then turned and looked at Leaphorn.

"Well now, I don't hardly know what to tell

you about that. If I had noticed you first, I'd have asked you the same thing."

Leaphorn laughed. "I probably would have told you I'm out here hunting quail. But then you'd have noticed this is a rifle and not something you use to shoot birds. And you wouldn't have believed me."

"Prob'ly not," Gershwin said. "I'd guess you were thinking about all that money taken out of that casino and how it had to be hidden someplace and maybe this old mine was it."

"Well," Leaphorn said, "it's true that the Navajo Nation doesn't offer high retirement pay. How about you? You looking for some extra unmarked paper money?"

"Are you talking as an officer of the law, or are you still a civilian?"

"I'm the same civilian you brought your list of names to," Leaphorn said. "Once you're out they don't let you back in."

"Well, then, I hope you have better luck than I did. There's no money back there. I turned over every piece of junk. Nothing. Just a waste of time." Gershwin started walking again.

"I heard some shots fired," Leaphorn said. "What was that about?"

Gershwin turned around and started back toward the mine. "Come on," he said. "I'll show you.

And I'll tell you, too. Remember me telling you I was pulling out. Going to move into a motel somewhere. Not wait around for those militia bastards to come after me. Well, I decided to hell with that. I'm too old a dog to let those punks run me out. I decided I'd have a showdown."

"Hold it a minute," Leaphorn said. "I want you to meet a friend of mine." He motioned to Chee.

Chee holstered his pistol, came out from behind the brush, raised a hand in greeting. If Gershwin was carrying a weapon it wasn't visible. If it was any size, he'd probably be carrying it under his belt, hidden by his shirt and not in a pocket. The sound of the gunshots suggested a serious weapon. Certainly not a pocket-size twenty-two.

"This is Sergeant Jim Chee," Leaphorn said. "Roy Gershwin."

Gershwin looked shocked. "Yes," he said, and nodded to Chee.

"Chee's short of money, too," Leaphorn said. "He's a single man, but he's trying to live on a police salary."

Gershwin gave Chee another look, nodded again, and resumed his walk toward the mine. "Well, as I was telling you, I drove out here thinking I was going to have it out with these bastards. Either take 'em in for the reward money, or run 'em off, or shoot 'em if I had to. That reward's supposed to be for dead or alive. I just decided not to run. I'm way too damned old to be running."

"You shot 'em?" Leaphorn asked.

"Just one. I shot Baker. George Ironhand, he got away."

They were in the structure by then, through a double doorway that pierced a partly tumbled wall and into the patterned light and darkness of a huge room. Sunlight streaming through gaps in its roof illuminated the cluttered earthen floor in streaks. It was about as Special Agent Cabot had described it. Empty except for a jumble of junk and scattered debris. Where the floor wasn't hidden by fallen roofing material and sheets of warped plywood, it was covered by layers of drifted sand, dust and trash drifted in by years of wind. Tumbleweeds were piled against the back wall, and beside them was the body of a man dressed in gray-green camouflage coveralls.

Gershwin gestured toward the body. "Baker," he said. "Son of a bitch tried to shoot me."

"Tell us about how it went," Leaphorn said.

"Well, I parked back there a ways so they wouldn't hear me coming. And walked up real quiet and looked in and that one"—Gershwin pointed to the body by the wall—"he seemed to be sleeping. The tall one was sitting over there, and when I came in he made a grab for his gun and I hollered for him to stop, but he got it, and then I shot him and he fell down. That woke up the other guy and he jumped up and pulled out a pistol and I hollered for him to drop it and he took a shot at me so I shot him, too."

"The first one you shot," Chee said. "Where did he go?"

"Be damned if I know," Gershwin said. "I thought he was down for good and I was busy with the other one, and when I was going to check on him, he wasn't there. I guess he just got out of here somehow. Didn't you fellas see him running away?"

"We didn't," Leaphorn said, "and we better be getting to our car. We need to call this in, and get the law out here to collect the body and get a search going for the one that got away."

"Surprised you didn't see him," Gershwin said.

"Where's your weapon?" Leaphorn asked. "You need to hand that over to Sergeant Chee here."

"I threw it away," Gershwin said. "I never had shot a man before, and when I realized what I'd done I just felt sick. Went to that side door over there and threw up and then I threw my pistol down in the canyon."

They had moved out through the broken doorway into the sunlight. Chee kept his hand near the butt of his pistol, thinking Leaphorn couldn't possibly believe that, thinking the weapon was probably a hand-gun and it was probably in the backpack Gershwin was carrying. Or perhaps stuck in Gershwin's belt, hidden by the shirt.

"It's a terrible feeling," Gershwin was saying, "shooting a man." And as he was saying that his hand flashed under the shirt and came out fumbling with a pistol.

Chee's pistol was pointed at Gershwin's chest. "Drop it," Chee said. "Drop it or I kill you."

Gershwin made an angry sound, dropped his pistol.

Leaphorn shouted, "Look out." There was a blast of sound from the darkness. Gershwin was knocked sprawling into the dirt.

"He's under that big sheet of plywood," Leaphorn shouted. "I saw a side of it rise. Then the muzzle flash."

The plywood was directly under the A-frame of timbers that rose through what was left of the building's roof. Chee and Leaphorn approached it as one approaches a prairie rattler, with caution. Chee did his stalking via the side door, a route with better cover. He got there first, motioned Leaphorn in. They stood on opposite sides of it, looking down at it.

"Gershwin is dead," Leaphorn said.

"I thought it looked like that," Chee said.

"If you pulled that plywood back, you'd expect to look right down into a vertical shaft," Leaphorn said. "But whoever pushed it up and stuck out that rifle barrel had to be standing on something."

"Probably some sort of rope ladder at least," Chee said. "Or maybe they dug out some sort of niche." He tried to visualize what would be under the plywood without much luck.

Leaphorn was studying him. "You want to pull it away and take a look?"

Chee laughed. "I think I'd rather just wait until Special Agent Cabot gets here with his people and let him do it. I wouldn't want to mess up the Bureau's crime scene."

TWENTY-NINE

JIM CHEE SPRAWLED across the rear seat of Unit 11, his throbbing ankle high on a pillow reminding him of what the doctor had said about putting weight on a sprain before it's healed. Otherwise, Chee was feeling no pain. He was at ease. He was content. True, George Ironhand was still at large in the canyons, either wounded or well, but he wasn't Chee's problem.

Chee relaxed, listened to the windshield wipers working against the off-and-on rain shower, eavesdropped now and then on the conversation the Legendary Lieutenant was having with Officer Manuelito (Leaphorn was calling her Bernie) and rehashing the events of a tense and tiring day.

The reinforcements had arrived a little before sundown. First came two big Federal Bureau of Investigation copters, hovering a while to find a place to put down among the hummocks of Mormon tea, the Special Agents swarming out, looking warlike in their official bulletproof costumes, pointing their automatic weapons at Leaphorn and looking miffed when Leaphorn ignored them. Then the business of trying to explain what had happened there. Explaining Gershwin to the Special Agent in Charge, who wanted to question everything, who wanted answers which would prove the Bureau was right in its Everett Jorie suicide/gang-leader conclusion, and who looked downright thunderstruck when he learned that the fellow instructing otherwise was just a civilian.

Chee grinned, remembering that. Leaphorn had cut off the SAC's arguments by suggesting he could end his doubts by sending a few of his troops over to Gershwin's truck and having them unpack some of the bundles, in which Leaphorn was confident they would find about one hundred seven pounds and eleven ounces of the paper money taken from the casino. The SAC did, and they did; some of the money was neatly double-sacked in eight of those Earth-Smart white-plastic kitchen trash bags stacked under Gershwin's luggage, and a bunch of the bigger bills was layered into the suitcases with his clothing. While that was happening the ground troops arrived—two sheriff's cars, a Utah State Police car and a BIA law-enforcement unit bringing an assortment of cops—including Border Patrol trackers with their dogs. The trackers nervously eyed the cumulus clouds, their tops backlit by the setting sun and their black bottoms producing lightning and promising the long-overdue rain. Trackers prefer daylight and dry ground and were making their preference obvious. Finally, the explaining stopped, an ambulance arrived to take away the much-photographed bodies, and now here Chee was, dry and comfortable, on his way home and an interested listener to the Legendary Lieutenant revealing a human side.

"I've only met her recently," Bernie was saying. "But she seemed very nice."

"An interesting person," Leaphorn said. "A real friend, I think." He chuckled. "At least she's willing to listen to me when I talk. When you're an old widower, and you haven't gotten used to living alone yet, that's something you need."

Which is why, Chee was thinking, *Leaphorn has been chattering like this.* He'd always thought of him as taciturn, hard to talk to. A silent man. But then Bernie was Bernie. He liked to talk to her, too. Or, come to think of it, he liked to talk while Bernie listened. He skipped backward into memories of conversations with Janet Pete. No problem there. Then came another memory, another comparison. Bernie putting ice on his swollen ankle, leaning over him, her soft hair brushing past his face. Janet kissing him. Janet's hair carried the perfume of flowers, Bernie's the scent of juniper and the wind.

"You don't seem old to me," Bernie was saying. "No older than my father, and he's still young."

"It's more than age," Leaphorn said. "Emma and I were married longer than you've been alive. One of those love-at-first-sight things when we were students at Arizona State. And when she died—" He didn't finish that.

The rain stopped. Bernie switched off the wipers. "I'll bet you she wouldn't have approved of you living alone, like a hermit. I'll bet she would want you to get married again."

Wow, Chee thought. *That took nerve. How will Lieutenant Leaphorn react to that?*

Leaphorn laughed. "Exactly. She did. But not Professor Bourebonette. At the hospital before her surgery she told me if anything went wrong, I should remember Navajo tradition."

"Marry her sister?" Bernie said. "You have a single sister-in-law?"

"Yep," Leaphorn said. "Emma almost always gave good advice, but her sister didn't like that idea any better than I did."

"I'll bet your wife would have approved of Professor Bourebonette," Bernie said. "I mean as your wife."

If Chee hadn't been watching while Bernie refused to surrender her sidearm to Leaphorn a few hours ago, he wouldn't have believed he was hearing this. He waited. Silence. Then Leaphorn said, "You know, Bernie, now you mention it, I'm sure she would."

What a woman, this Officer Bernadette Manuelito. Chee remembered the sort of subconscious uneasiness he'd felt when Bernie showed up at his trailer and asked him to help her wounded boyfriend. It was jealousy, of course, though he didn't want to admit it then. And he was feeling it again now.

"Bernie," Chee said, "what's the condition report on Teddy Bai?"

"Much better," Bernie said.

"Did you talk to him?"

"Rosemary did," she said. "She said he's going to be well enough so they won't have to postpone their wedding."

"Well, now," Chee said. "Wow. That's really good news." And he meant it.

As Tony's home state paper,
the *Oklahoma City Oklahoman,* says,
"Readers who have not discovered Hillerman
should not waste one minute more."
Find out what you've been missing
with Leaphorn and Chee . . .

A dead reporter's secret notebook implicates a senatorial candidate and political figures in a million-dollar murder scam.

THE FLY ON THE WALL

John Cotton was a simple man with one desire: to write the greatest story of his life and have enough life left to read all about it. He knows what to do when he finds a great story, but he is a little afraid when a big story begins to find him. It starts when a fellow reporter is murdered, and his notebook, filled with information about a tax scam, ends up in John's hands. Not long afterward, a body is discovered in John's car. Then John's car ends up in the river, a bomb is found in his apartment, and his girlfriend drops out of sight. It's up to John to unravel the mystery of the notebook and why anyone would kill for the information it contains.

"Fascinating . . . breathless suspense."
Minneapolis Tribune

"Explosive . . . sensational . . . excellent."
Cleveland Plain Dealer

An archaeological dig, a steel hypodermic needle, and the strange laws of the Zuñi complicate the disappearance of two young boys.

DANCE HALL OF THE DEAD

Two young boys suddenly disappear. One of them, a Zuñi, leaves a pool of blood behind. Lieutenant Joe Leaphorn of the Navajo Tribal Police tracks the brutal killer. Three things complicate the search: an archaeological dig, a steel hypodermic needle, and the strange laws of the Zuñi. Compelling, terrifying, and highly suspenseful, *Dance Hall of the Dead* never relents from first page till last.

"High entertainment, an aesthetically
satisfying glimpse of the
still-powerful tribal mysteries."
New York Times

"Riveting descriptions of Zuñi religious rites."
Newsweek

A baffling investigation of murder, ghosts, and witches can be solved only by Lieutenant Leaphorn, a man who understands both his own people and cold-blooded killers.

LISTENING WOMAN

The state police and FBI are baffled when an old man and a teenage girl are brutally murdered. The blind Navajo Listening Woman speaks of ghosts and of witches. But Lieutenant Leaphorn of the Navajo Tribal Police knows his people as well as he knows cold-blooded killers. His incredible investigation carries him from a dead man's secret to a kidnap scheme, to a conspiracy that stretches back more than one hundred years. Leaphorn arrives at the threshold of a solution—and is greeted with the most violent confrontation of his career.

"Hillerman's mysteries are special . . .
Listening Woman is among the best."
Washington Post

"A good exciting mystery that has everything."
Pittsburgh Press

An assassin waits for Officer Chee in the desert to protect a vision of death that for thirty years has been fed by greed and washed in blood.

PEOPLE OF DARKNESS

Who would murder a dying man? Why would someone steal a box of rocks? And why would a rich man's wife pay $3,000 to get them back? These questions haunt Sergeant Jim Chee of the Navajo Tribal Police as he journeys into the scorching Southwest. But there, out in the Bad Country, a lone assassin waits for Chee to come seeking answers, waits ready and willing to protect a vision of death that for thirty years has been fed by greed and washed in blood.

"Hillerman . . . is in a class by himself."
Los Angeles Times

"Great suspense."
Chicago Tribune

Sergeant Jim Chee becomes trapped in a deadly web of a cunningly spun plot driven by Navajo sorcery and white man's greed.

THE DARK WIND

A corpse whose palms and soles have been "scalped" is only the first in a series of disturbing clues: an airplane's mysterious crash in the nighttime desert, a bizarre attack on a windmill, a vanishing shipment of cocaine. Sergeant Jim Chee of the Navajo Tribal Police is trapped in a deadly web of a cunningly spun plot driven by Navajo sorcery and white man's greed.

"Hillerman is first-rate . . . fresh, original,
and highly suspenseful."
Los Angeles Times

"A beauty of a thriller . . .
exotic and compelling reading."
Cleveland Plain Dealer

A photo sends Officer Chee on an odyssey of murder and revenge that moves from an Indian hogan to a deadly healing ceremony.

THE GHOSTWAY

Old Joseph Joe sees it all. Two strangers spill blood at the Shiprock Wash-O-Mat. One dies. The other drives off into the dry lands of the Big Reservation, but not before he shows the old Navajo a photo of the man he seeks. This is enough to send Tribal Policeman Jim Chee after a killer ... and on an odyssey of murder and revenge that moves from an Indian hogan and its trapped ghost, to the dark underbelly of L.A., to a healing ceremony whose cure could be death.

"A first-rate story of suspense and mystery."
The New Yorker

"Fresh, original and highly suspenseful."
Los Angeles Times

Three shotgun blasts in a trailer bring Officer Chee and Lieutenant Leaphorn together for the first time in an investigation of ritual, witchcraft, and blood.

SKINWALKERS

Three shotgun blasts explode into the trailer of Officer Jim Chee of the Navajo Tribal Police. But Chee survives to join partner Lieutenant Joe Leaphorn in a frightening investigation that takes them into a dark world of ritual, witchcraft, and blood—all tied to the elusive and evil "skinwalker." Brimming with Navajo lore and sizzling suspense, *Skinwalkers* brings Chee and Leaphorn, Hillerman's best-selling detective team, together for the first time.

"Full of mystery, intrigue, and
dangerous magic."
Ross Thomas

"Hillerman is unique and *Skinwalkers*
is one of his best."
Los Angeles Times

Stolen ancient goods and new corpses at an ancient burial site confound Leaphorn and Chee. They must plunge into the past to unearth the truth.

A THIEF OF TIME

A noted anthropologist vanishes at a moonlit Indian ruin where "thieves of time" ravage sacred ground for profit. When two corpses appear amid stolen goods and bones at an ancient burial site, Navajo Tribal Policemen Lieutenant Joe Leaphorn and Officer Jim Chee must plunge into the past to unearth the astonishing truth behind a mystifying series of horrific murders.

"Skillful. Provocative. The action never flags."
New York Times Book Review

"Vintage Tony Hillerman: suspenseful, compelling! Hillerman transcends the mystery genre and this is one of [his] best."
Washington Post Book World

A grave robber and a corpse reunite Leaphorn and Chee in a dangerous arena of superstition, ancient ceremony, and living gods.

TALKING GOD

As Leaphorn seeks the identity of a murder victim, Chee is arresting Smithsonian conservator Henry Highhawk for ransacking the sacred bones of his ancestors. As the layers of each case are peeled away, it becomes shockingly clear that they are connected, that there are mysterious others pursuing Highhawk, and that Leaphorn and Chee have entered into the dangerous arena of superstition, ancient ceremony, and living gods.

"Woven as tightly as a Navajo blanket."
Newsweek

"Suddenly now Hillerman has become a
national literary and cultural sensation . . .
it does not take too much to determine why
Hillerman has become so popular. He is a
solid, down-to-earth storyteller."
Los Angeles Times

*When a bullet kills Officer Jim Chee's good friend
Del, a Navajo shaman is arrested for homicide, but
the case is far from closed.*

COYOTE WAITS

The car fire didn't kill Navajo Tribal Policeman Del-
bert Nez, a bullet did. Officer Jim Chee's good friend
Del lies dead, and a whiskey-soaked Navajo shaman
is found with the murder weapon. The old man is
Ashie Pinto. He's quickly arrested for homicide and
defended by a woman Chee could either love or loathe.
But when Pinto won't utter a word of confession or
denial, Lieutenant Joe Leaphorn begins an investigation. Soon, Leaphorn and Chee unravel a complex plot
of death involving a historical find, a lost fortune . . .
and the mythical Coyote, who is always waiting, and
always hungry.

> "Hillerman is at the top of his form
> in *Coyote Waits*."
> *San Francisco Chronicle*

> "The master's newest Chee-Leaphorn
> mystery with the usual informative
> Navajo anthropology."
> *Book News*

Officer Chee attempts to solve two modern murders by deciphering the sacred clowns' ancient message to the people of the Tano pueblo.

SACRED CLOWNS

During a Tano kachina ceremony, something in the antics of the dancing *koshare* fills the air with tension. Moments later the clown is found brutally bludgeoned in the same manner that a reservation schoolteacher was killed just days before.

In true Navajo style, Officer Jim Chee and Lieutenant Leaphorn of the Navajo Tribal Police go back to the beginning to decipher the sacred clowns' message to the people of the Tano pueblo. Amid guarded tribal secrets and crooked Indian traders, they find a trail of blood that links a runaway schoolboy, two dead bodies, and the mysterious presence of a sacred artifact.

"This is Hillerman at his best, mixing human nature, ethnicity and the overpowering physical presence of the Southwest."
Newsweek

"[Hillerman's] affection for his characters and for the real world in which they live and work has never been more appealingly demonstrated."
Los Angeles Times Book Review

A man met his death on Ship Rock Mountain eleven years ago, and with the discovery of his body by a group of climbers, Chee and Leaphorn must hunt down the cause of his lonely death.

THE FALLEN MAN

Sprawled on a ledge under the peak of Ship Rock Mountain for eleven years lies an unknown body, now only bones. At Canyon de Chelly, three hundred miles across the Navajo reservation, a sniper shoots an old canyon guide who has always walked that pollen path in peace. At his home in Window Rock, Joe Leaphorn, newly retired from the Navajo Tribal Police, connects skeleton and sniper, and remembers an old puzzle he could never solve. At his office in Shiprock, Acting Lieutenant Jim Chee is too busy to take much interest in the case—until it hits too close to home. Bringing the beauty and mystery of the Southwest to vivid life once again, Tony Hillerman has reunited Joe Leaphorn and Jim Chee in an evocative mystery in which the past and the present join forces in a most unholy union.

"The personal tensions add another facet to the story, which continues the author's fascination with the savagery that men do to themselves and to the land they claim to hold sacred."
New York Times Book Review

When Acting Lieutenant Jim Chee catches a Hopi poacher huddled over a butchered Navajo Tribal Police officer, he has an open-and-shut case—until his former boss, Joe Leaphorn, blows it wide open.

THE FIRST EAGLE

Now retired from the Navajo Tribal Police, Leaphorn has been hired to find a hot-headed female biologist hunting for the key to a virulent plague lurking in the Southwest. The scientist disappeared from the same area the same day the Navajo cop was murdered. Is she a suspect or another victim? And what about a report that a skinwalker—a Navajo witch—was seen at the same time and place too? For Leaphorn and Chee, the answers lie buried in a complicated knot of superstition and science, in a place where the worlds of native peoples and outside forces converge and collide.

"Surrendering to Hillerman's strong narrative voice and supple storytelling techniques, we come to see that ancient cultures and modern sciences are simply different mythologies for the same reality."
New York Times Book Review

Hunting Badger *finds Navajo Tribal Police officers Joe Leaphorn and Jim Chee working two angles of the same case—each trying to catch the right-wing militiamen who pulled off a violent heist at an Indian casino.*

HUNTING BADGER

Three armed men raid the Ute tribe's gambling casino, and then disappear in the maze of canyons on the Utah-Arizona border. The FBI takes over the investigation, and agents swarm in with helicopters and high-tech equipment. Making an explosive situation even hotter, these experts devise a theory of the crime that makes a wounded deputy sheriff a suspect — a development that brings in Tribal Police Sergeant Jim Chee and his longtime colleague, retired Lieutenant Joe Leaphorn, to help.

Chee finds a fatal flaw in the federal theory and Leaphorn sees an intriguing pattern connecting this crime with the exploits of a legendary Ute hero bandit. Balancing politics, outsiders, and missing armed fugitives, Leaphorn and Chee soon find themselves caught in the most perplexing—and deadly—crime hunt of their lives . . .

"Hillerman soars."
Boston Globe

"Hillerman continues to dazzle . . .
A standout."
Washington Post Book World

A haunting tale of obsessive greed—of lost love and murder—as only the master, Tony Hillerman, can tell it.

THE WAILING WIND

Officer Bernadette Manuelito found the dead man slumped over the cab of a blue pickup abandoned in a dry gulch off a dirt road—with a rich ex-con's phone number in his pocket and a tobacco tin filled with tracer gold. It's her initial mishandling of the scene that spells trouble for her supervisor, Sergeant Jim Chee of the Navajo Tribal Police—but it's the echoes of a long-ago crime scene that call the legendary former Lieutenant Joe Leaphorn out of retirement. Years earlier, Leaphorn followed the trail of a beautiful, young, and missing wife to a dead end, and his failure has haunted him ever since. But ghosts never sleep in these high, lonely Southwestern hills. And the twisted threads of craven murders past and current may finally be coming together, thanks to secrets once moaned in torment on the desert wind.

"Enough to give anyone the shivers."
New York Times Book Review

"Grade A . . . Thrilling, chilling . . .
another Hillerman treasure."
Denver Rocky Mountain News

Leaphorn and Chee must battle the feds and a clever killer in a case that will take them from the tribe's Four Corners country all the way south to the Mexican border and the Sonoran Desert.

THE SINISTER PIG

Sergeant Jim Chee is troubled by the nameless corpse discovered just inside his jurisdiction, at the edge of the Jicarilla Apache natural gas field. More troubling still is the FBI's insistence that the Bureau take over the case, calling the unidentified victim's death a "hunting accident."

But if a hunter was involved, Chee knows the prey was intentionally human. This belief is shared by the legendary Lieutenant Joe Leaphorn, who once again is pulled out of retirement by the possibility of serious wrongs being committed against the Navajo nation by the Washington bureaucracy. Yet it is former policewoman Bernadette Manuelito, recently relocated to Customs Patrol at the U.S.-Mexico border, who possibly holds the key to a fiendishly twisted conspiracy of greed, lies, and murder—and whose only hope for survival now rests in the hands of friends too far away for comfort.

"Riveting . . . This *Pig* flies!"
People

"An extraordinary display of
sheer plotting craftsmanship."
New York Times Book Review

*In 1956, an airplane crash left the remains of 172
passengers scattered among the majestic cliffs of
the Grand Canyon—including an arm attached to a
briefcase containing a fortune in gems. Half a century later, one of the missing diamonds has reappeared . . . and the wolves are on the scent.*

SKELETON MAN

Former Navajo Tribal Police Lieutenant Joe Leaphorn is
coming out of retirement to help exonerate a slow, simple kid accused of robbing a trading post. Billy Tuve
claims he received the diamond he tried to pawn from
a mysterious old man in the canyon, and his story has
attracted the dangerous attention of strangers to the
Navajo land—one more interested in a severed limb
than in the fortune it was handcuffed to, another willing to murder to keep lost secrets hidden. But nature
herself may prove the deadliest adversary, as Leaphorn
and Sergeant Jim Chee follow a puzzle—and a killer—
down into the dark realm of Skeleton Man.

"Top-notch . . . A yarn well spun."
New York Daily News

"Bestselling author Tony Hillerman . . . is back
in top form . . . One of Hillerman's strongest
mysteries in an exceptional career."
Santa Fe New Mexican

Retirement has never sat well with former Navajo Tribal Police Lieutenant Joe Leaphorn. Now the ghosts of a still-unsolved case are returning to haunt him . . .

THE SHAPE SHIFTER

Joe Leaphorn's interest in the case is reawakened by a photograph in a magazine spread of a one-of-a-kind Navajo rug—a priceless work of woven art that was supposedly destroyed in a suspicious fire many years earlier. The rug, commemorating one of the darkest and most terrible chapters in American history, was always said to be cursed, and now the friend who brought it to Leaphorn's attention has mysteriously gone missing.

With newly wedded officers Jim Chee and Bernie Manuelito just back from their honeymoon, the legendary ex-lawman is on his own to pick up the threads of a crime he'd once thought impossible to untangle. And they're leading him back into a world of lethal greed, shifting truths, and changing faces, where a cold-blooded killer still resides.

"Hillerman scores. . . . Atmospheric and suspenseful. . . . With *The Shape Shifter*, Hillerman once again proves himself the master of Southwest mystery fiction."
Santa Fe New Mexican

NEW YORK TIMES BESTSELLING AUTHOR

TONY HILLERMAN

THE SHAPE SHIFTER

978-0-06-056347-9

The ghosts of former Navajo Tribal Police Lieutenant Joe Leaphorn's last, still unsolved case are returning to haunt him.

SKELETON MAN

978-0-06-196779-5

Half a century after a fatal plane crash a diamond from a briefcase one of the passengers carried has reappeared.

THE WAILING WIND

978-0-06-196781-8

Officer Bernadette Manuelito found the dead man slumped over in an abandoned pickup truck with a tobacco tin filled with tracer gold nearby.

THE SINISTER PIG

978-0-06-201804-5

The possibility of serious wrongs being committed by the Washington bureaucracy against the Navajo nation brings Leaphorn and Chee together after a man's death is ruled a "hunting accident."

www.tonyhillermanbooks.com

Visit www.AuthorTracker.com for exclusive information on your favorite HarperCollins authors.

Available wherever books are sold or please call 1-800-331-3761 to order.

THL1 0711

NEW YORK TIMES BESTSELLING AUTHOR

TONY HILLERMAN

HUNTING BADGER
978-0-06-196782-5

Navajo Tribal police officers Joe Leaphorn and Jim Chee are working two angles of the same case—each trying to catch the right-wing militiamen who pulled off a violent heist at an Indian casino.

COYOTE WAITS
978-0-06-180837-1
See it on PBS *Mystery!*
When a bullet kills Officer Jim Chee's good friend Del, a Navajo shaman is arrested for homicide, but the case is far from closed.

FINDING MOON
978-0-06-206843-9

Moon Mathias discovers his dead brother's baby daughter is waiting for him in Southeast Asia—a child he didn't know existed. Finding her in the aftermath of the war brings out a side of Moon he had forgotten he possessed.

THE FALLEN MAN
978-0-06-196777-1

A man met his death on Ship Rock Mountain eleven years ago, and with the discovery of his body by a group of climbers, Chee and Leaphorn must hunt down the cause of his lonely death.

THE FIRST EAGLE
978-0-06-196780-1

When acting Lt. Jim Chee catches a Hopi poacher over a butchered Navajo Tribal police officer, he has an open-and-shut case—until his former boss, Joe Leaphorn, blows it wide open.

www.tonyhillermanbooks.com

Visit www.AuthorTracker.com for exclusive information on your favorite HarperCollins authors.

Available wherever books are sold or please call 1-800-331-3761 to order.

THL2 0711

MASTERWORKS OF MYSTERY AND SUSPENSE FROM
NEW YORK TIMES BESTSELLING AUTHOR

TONY HILLERMAN

"HILLERMAN TRANSCENDS THE MYSTERY GENRE!"
Washington Post Book World

THE FLY ON THE WALL
978-0-06-206844-6

A dead reporter's secret notebook implicates a senatorial candidate
and other political figures in a million-dollar murder scam.

SKINWALKERS
978-0-06-201811-3
See it on PBS *Mystery!*

Three shotgun blasts bring Officer Chee and Lt. Leaphorn together
for the first time in an investigation of ritual, witchcraft, and blood.

TALKING GOD
978-0-06-196783-2

A grave robber and a corpse reunite Leaphorn and Chee in a
dangerous arena of superstition, ancient ceremony, and living gods.

THE GHOSTWAY
978-0-06-196778-8

A photo sends Officer Chee on an odyssey of murder and revenge that
moves from an Indian hogan to a deadly healing ceremony.

SACRED CLOWNS
978-0-06-180836-4

Officer Chee attempts to solve two modern murders by deciphering
the sacred clown's ancient message to the people of the Tano pueblo.

www.tonyhillermanbooks.com

Visit www.AuthorTracker.com for exclusive
information on your favorite HarperCollins authors.

Available wherever books are sold or please call 1-800-331-3761 to order.
THL3 0711

MASTERWORKS OF MYSTERY AND SUSPENSE FROM
NEW YORK TIMES BESTSELLING AUTHOR

TONY HILLERMAN

THE BLESSING WAY
978-0-06-180835-7

Lt. Joe Leaphorn must stalk a supernatural killer known as
the "Wolfwitch" along a chilling trail of mysticism and murder.

A THIEF OF TIME
See it on PBS *Mystery!*
978-0-06-180840-1

When two corpses appear amid stolen goods and bones from an ancient burial
site, Leaphorn and Chee must plunge into the past to unearth the truth.

DANCE HALL OF THE DEAD
978-0-06-180838-8

An archaeological dig, a steel hypodermic needle, and the strange laws
of the Zuni complicate the disappearance of two young boys.

THE DARK WIND
978-0-06-201802-1

Sgt. Jim Chee becomes trapped in the deadly web of a cunningly spun
plot driven by Navajo sorcery and white man's greed.

LISTENING WOMAN
978-0-06-196776-4

A baffling investigation of murder, ghosts, and witches can be solved only
by Lt. Joe Leaphorn, a man who understands both his own people
and the cold-blooded killers.

PEOPLE OF DARKNESS
978-0-06-180839-5

An assassin waits for Officer Chee in the desert to protect a vision of
death that for thirty years has been fed by greed and washed with blood.

www.tonyhillermanbooks.com

Visit www.AuthorTracker.com for exclusive
information on your favorite HarperCollins authors.

Available wherever books are sold or please call 1-800-331-3761 to order.

THL4 0711